COLLECTION MANAGEMENT

How to Make a Bird

MARTINE MURRAY

 Arthur A. Levine Books / An Imprint of Scholastic Inc.

Special thanks to Rosalind Price and Sue Flockhart; thanks also to Antoni Jach and Tim Freedman; and to the Tasmanian Writers' Center for my residency there.

Text and illustrations copyright © 2003 by Martine Murray • All rights reserved. Published by Arthur A. Levine Books, an imprint of Scholastic Inc., *Publishers since 1920*, by arrangement with Allen & Unwin Pty. Ltd., Sydney, Australia. SCHOLASTIC and the LANTERN LOGO are trademarks and/or registered trademarks of Scholastic Inc. • No part of this publication may be reproduced, stored in a retrieval system, or transmitted in any form or by any means, electronic, mechanical, photocopying, recording, or otherwise, without written permission of the publisher. For information regarding permission, write to Scholastic Inc., Attention: Permissions Department, 557 Broadway, New York, NY 10012. • Library of Congress Cataloging-in-Publication Data • Murray, Martine. • How to make a bird / Martine Murray. — 1st American ed. • p. cm. • Summary: When seventeen-year-old, small-town Australian girl Manon Clarkeson leaves home in the middle of the night, wearing her mother's long, inappropriate red silk dress and riding her bike, she is heading for Melbourne, not exactly sure what she is looking for but not wanting to stay at home alone with her father anymore. • ISBN 978-0-439-66951-1 (hardcover : alk. paper) [1. Runaways — Fiction. 2. Emotional problems — Fiction. 3. Family problems — Fiction. 4. Mothers — Fiction. 5. Brothers and sisters — Fiction. 6. Grief — Fiction. 7. Australia — Fiction.] I. Title. • PZ7.M9637Ho 2010 • [Fic] — dc22 • 2009027453 • 10 9 8 7 6 5 4 3 2 1   10 11 12 13 14 • Printed in the U.S.A. 23 • First American edition, June 2010 • Book design by Elizabeth B. Parisi and Kristina Albertson

In memory of Lise

and

For John

A LIST OF THINGS
YOU MIGHT NOT HEAR.

eyelash opening on the pillow
the appearance of a star.
a leaf leaving a tree
a hand in your hair
a lie being withheld
a tear's journey from eye to shoe
air becoming blue
longing

———————

chapter one

There are these wings and they're in the sky. They're pointing downward, like a pair of stiff old socks left on the line. If you were the kind of person who had dramatic tendencies, you'd think a nearby angel, who'd been hovering over Blackjack Road, had torn off her wings in despair and left them hanging in the sky as a warning.

But I knew the wings weren't made of angel, or bird either. I knew they were only balsa wood, and I knew it was Mr. Nelson who had strung them up there, because I saw him do it. The wings once belonged to a balsa-wood eagle, fixed in the sky in a permanent swoop position to scare the birds off Mr. Nelson's apples. It was a glorious Hollywood position for the wings, outstretched and looming above the world, lording it up, presiding. So, once the body went and the wings drooped, you couldn't help feeling despair on behalf of the wings. You couldn't help noticing they weren't looking so exultant anymore. And you couldn't help thinking that anyone else who saw those old wings might even laugh at them, or think they were just a fudged-up kids' kite.

It was on account of those despairing wings that I didn't make a clean getaway. It was dark when I left, so I couldn't actually see them, but I knew they were there, flapping in a stricken, dying-fish way. I yanked my bike out of the garage and was just ready to ride off into the night when, in my mind, those wings started their death flap. I tried to be kind of tough about it, but there was no denying that the wings had put a sad feeling in me. I got so edgy I had to stand still and look about for a while. The moon was lying pale and quivery in the sky, like a bony finger mark on a black cloth. The houses were hushed and still and I was telling myself there was no reason to feel sad, not even for the wings, or the way the moon was fading, getting thin like tissue. There wasn't even one piece of brightness to ache over. The fields were like crinkled-up gray blankets huddled over a sleeping earth. Harry Jacob's house looked grim, all bitten by the blackness. During the day it was the color of a mint chew, and perched awkwardly on its bald grass slope as if it hadn't quite settled. Now it had sunk smugly into the night's shadows and it peered down at me as if it knew what I was doing, standing there alone in the darkness. In the midst of the bleating crickets and cracking thin limbs of trees, I could almost hear the house letting out a muffled sneery snort, like my mother used to when I said what I thought of one thing or another.

Well, don't pretend, I felt like saying to Harry Jacob's green house, don't pretend that you belong now. Just because the night has made you the same color as all the other houses, don't pretend to be serious, because as soon as the light comes up you'll still be an old green house that doesn't look right.

I turned away from Harry's house and pulled up my dress so I could hitch my leg over the bike. Eddie would have been appalled if he'd seen me trying to ride a bike in this long dress. It was stupid, but I didn't care. I was even glad it was stupid.

Our house was the kind that did look right. You didn't need to feel embarrassed about our house, with its bullnose veranda and white weatherboards and some of my mother's English roses frothing up the side. There were two identical windows at the front, which made it look balanced and polite, like a face that would never shriek or contort in pain. I felt funny, thinking about the way the house looked on the outside and the way it felt on the inside, how they didn't match, how trying to match them up was like trying to wear a dress inside out and make it look right. I went all tight and elbowy just thinking about it. Anyone else would feel certain that this was a house with a piano in it, and someone sitting at a table with a napkin on their knee, and someone else humming or stitching up a hole in a faithful old jumper, or rising out of an armchair to make tea. I tried to fix this outside picture of the house in my mind, as if its calm, unshakable face were true. And with that picture in my mind I really would have ridden off, if it wasn't for the thing I felt. It came over me with a huge overlapping quiet, coming right out of the darkness. Not from the house, but out of the pure dark air. It wasn't the wings anymore, it was almost a noise . . . but not quite, more the sense that a noise was waiting, twitching like a long-eared animal in a burrow. I could tell that the noise, if it came, would not belong to the normal soft hum of leaves scraping the air.

I turned quickly and looked behind me.

Harry Jacob stood on the grass. He looked unnatural and dark and struck dead still, standing there in pale pajamas that quivered around his legs. His head tilted a little to one side.

"Hey, you scared me, Harry," I called out in a loud whisper. "What the hell are you doing?"

Harry took a few steps toward me and leaned up against the fence post. He had that look he gets when he can't understand something and all the thinking parts in his mind crash up against each other and break down. I didn't like looking at his broken-down face; it made me mad.

"Well, what are *you* doing, Mannie? Where the hell are you going at this time? It's five o'clock in the morning. And why are you wearing that dress?"

I looked down at the dress, in a purposefully weary and innocent way, as if to ascertain what dress I was wearing.

It was the red one. We both knew it was.

"It's my mother's dress."

"Why are you wearing it?"

"'Cause I just am. I'm celebrating." I could feel my bottom lip bloat up like a bullfrog.

"Celebrating what?" Harry looked down and kicked at the

4

grass with his bare foot. There hadn't been much to celebrate lately.

"Anything. The sound of a train coming. You've gotta find something to celebrate." I pushed my hands in the air because I felt like throwing something away, only I had nothing to throw.

"Where you going? You can't ride a bike in that dress."

"Yeah? Watch me!" I twisted the long part of the dress up and held it over the handlebars, to show him how it was done. Harry came closer and stood in front of me.

"You can see your legs," he said, and then he smiled, "right up to your undies."

Hell, I liked that smile he had. Just half his mouth went up, and he looked lopsided and sweet. But I wasn't going to smile back. I didn't want the conversation to get soft.

"Who cares? Who's gonna see anything out here at this time?" My head tipped back and I heard my own mean laugh empty into the night. I didn't want to look at Harry. "I'm going to Melbourne. Not just to visit. I've got some business there, and then I'm just gonna see. Who knows? I may even go someplace else. Sydney. Or Paris even."

He just stood there, nodding his head, with his arms folded across his chest and his eyes looking down. I had planned it so that there wouldn't have to be any explanations or good-byes, and now Harry had stuffed up my plan by appearing, all struck and weird in the night, when he should have been sleeping.

"Were you spying on me, Harry?"

"Shit, Mannie, you know I wasn't spying. I just wasn't asleep and I heard your garage opening. I looked out — in case it was someone, you know, breaking in — and I saw you, just standing there in that dress, and I thought . . . Well, I don't know what I thought."

He ran his hand through his hair and it parted over his forehead. I almost stretched out my hand to smooth it back how I liked it best. Harry has brown curls in his hair, and when they sit right on his face he looks a certain way, like a lovely grown child, like someone who could never ever do an evil thing or think a mean thought. Now that he had pushed the hair off his face, it didn't look as good, and I knew I was right to leave. Besides, Harry always wore the same old clothes.

"You know what? The problem is, we're different. You're slow and I'm fast. It's like we're in a different race, you and me." I didn't mean to say it like that. Sometimes sentences rushed out before I checked them over for holes or hidden weapons.

Harry took a step back, as if he was jolted by the force of the mean words I was saying. He turned and stared out over the fields, but you could tell he wasn't seeing the view.

"The problem is, I'm not in any race." He was shaking his head as if he was sort of disgusted, like the air smelled bad. "So you do what you like, Mannie?" He didn't look at me. He just threw the words out, as if they were rotten inside him.

The night seemed to be fading around us. I sighed and fixed my eyes on the moon. It should just give up and go away and let the sun come, I thought. Then I adjusted my pack in the basket, not because it needed adjusting, but because something needed doing. After a while Harry spoke.

"Does your dad know?" His look was hard and it made me worry. Harry never looked hard. I shook my head.

"Course he doesn't. That's why I'm creeping out now. I'm going to ride to Castlemaine and catch the first train in the morning. Don't make me feel bad about this, Harry."

He was turning away, and just watching him turn away like that was making me feel bad. In fact everything he did was making me feel bad and I was angry about it. I was just about to charge at him when he looked back, with his arm raised as if in a final salute, so I could only see half his face, and that was clouded by darkness.

"Hope you win your race," he called out. But you couldn't tell if he really meant it or if he meant the exact opposite. And then he was walking away. Just like that: one, two, three.

If there was one thing that really annoyed me, it was someone walking away on me. I dropped my bike, but still he didn't turn. I ran up to him and pulled at his wrist.

"Well, aren't you even going to say good-bye? Harry?" My voice rose and stumbled out of me. He was looking down at my hand around his wrist, as if my hand was taking liberties and no longer had a right to be there. I dropped his wrist and frowned.

"Good-bye, Mannie." His pajamas shivered around him.

"Bye, Harry." I touched his arm, just slightly. Then I turned and went, and I didn't think once about those old wings.

chapter two

It was a twenty-eight-minute bike ride to the train station, if you took the highway. Usually I went up Chanters Lane, and then along Specimen Gully Road, but at night it was too dark to see the potholes. Every day I walked up that thin snake of a road, so I knew the lane pretty well. I knew its turns and slopes, the rasping sound it made, the whipped-up long grass beside it, and the gullies all choked with bullrush and thistle. You could probably hear my hungry old thoughts still sifting through those thistles. Every day I'd trodden them in and then stirred them up; because of them, I'd heard my heart going *thump thump thump* like a wallaby bounding through the bush.

If you think about it, you can see your whole life worn into the slant and cut of the land. You're part of what trod it into the shape it's in; you and the cows and the wind, and the storm of your own longings too. So you're in it: the line and the weight of you, the momentum you unrolled like a stone on the slope, the directions you chose or the paths that chose you. You're in it and it's in you.

You can tell the land has a hold on you when a pair of forgotten wings gets into your head and your mind starts yelping. I'd been up that road enough. It was my old way. Besides, it was a dirt lane and I didn't want to ruin my dress. I wasn't in a good mood anymore, not after seeing Harry. He'd made me feel bad, and I needed to concentrate on cleaning him out of my mind. So I rode along the highway, where it was flat.

I took my hands off the handlebars and stuck them behind my head for a minute, riding just like Eddie did when he was showing off around girls. If anyone had seen me they would have said, "Well, I never! There goes Mannie Clarkeson, on a deserted highway, riding no-hands in the dark, in a long red dress that's blowing out behind her like a sail." I was showing off to no one, except the moon. I was making myself feel like a champion, like a winner, like someone who was bursting through the finish line in a big stadium. I was swallowing the wind and the darkness around me, and all the unheard opinions too. It was a lot of work, and I wasn't quite convinced. I guess that's why I had the red dress on: to make me more convincing.

The red dress was my mother's, made of satin or silk or something that shone. At the front there were three tiny black buttons, and from the waist it widened and floated down. It made me feel tremendously elegant and worthwhile. I wanted to keep that feeling. When Mum wore it she seemed to shine, not with light, but with some deep, dark color. It was a kind of blood glowing and it made you want to be near her, just as you want to be near shafts of winter sun, thinking they might warm you.

But those were the times when we had guests. Mum would have a glass of wine in her hand, and she'd be smiling and laughing just like a lady in a magazine advertising cigarettes or shoes.

Dad organized the parties, because he knew it cheered her up. He'd ask the Brixtons, old Ted Ballard, Mr. and Mrs. Jacob, and sometimes the Bartholomews or the Hill family or Travis Houghton. Dad would be handing out drinks and relaxing his smile and gazing over at his foreign wife, checking to make sure she was happy. She sat with one hand on the back of the couch and one foot poking out, playing with the edge of the red dress, making it billow and lap like a spilling wave. She spoke of Paris and the famous Théâtre Pigalle, where she had been an actress. Everyone watched her, because of the dress and the way her hands conducted the air. When she laughed, one hand went to her mouth as if to stop the laugh tumbling out, even though she wanted everyone to hear it. Her face lifted up, and she smiled afterward because she knew how she had drawn everyone toward her with that bubbling-out laugh.

At some point in those evenings, Mum would request music and call for Eddie.

"Eddie, Eddie, let's dance. You and I." She would hold her hand out and Eddie would frown and push his arms into the couch, as if he was digging himself into it. "Eddie," she'd plead, "please dance with me. Come on. Just one dance? For your mother?"

Eddie would stare at the floor. I remember once how the room waited, how it seemed as if time couldn't move at all but was trapped, wedged up in the space between Mum's pleading hand and Eddie, sitting stiff and reluctant as a fence post. Everyone was watching. Our mother's hand was the only thing that moved. Her wrist was limp and the hand fluttered at Eddie. It made you feel that Eddie had to take hold of the hand, had to.

I didn't like it: the way Eddie and Mum together made this big tear in the night's fabric, a gaping hole with everyone shifting and getting uncomfortable and thinking bad thoughts. Mr. Bartholomew was rubbing his eyebrow, and Travis Houghton was grinning and sitting with his arms spread across the back of the old couch. Dad creased his body toward the record player, with one hand on the volume button, staring at Eddie and at Mum's pleading hand with a great pain in his eyes. But then Mrs. Nelson, who had a big heaving bust, let out a breath as Eddie slowly pushed himself up and, with his head hung down, dragged his feet over and caught the flapping hand. And as he did, the music welled up and filled the room and poured over the stiffness, and there was a melting, a sinking, a swaying, as everyone watched the dancing pair. They swung in and out, and Eddie hardly tried. He didn't make any little fancy movements, but he could do the steps. She'd taught him. Just so she could do all the fancy stuff. She was like a ribbon whirling around him. Eddie, her perfect dark center.

She was never happier. Her face was open and her eyes hovered like dark moths, as if for once she wasn't aware of who was watching. She didn't even toss a smile at Travis Houghton. She moved like an angel, weightless and soft. She always said that Dad had two left feet, but Eddie was just like her, a natural.

It was true. She and Eddie were both light on their feet. They drew people toward them, not because of how they looked or what they said, but because of the way they moved: that slow, easy slipping, both of them filling a space the way honey sinks into a bowl. And she spoke with a voice that unraveled over you. Eddie had that as well — a deep lovely voice. Only Eddie didn't use his voice to make you do things for him, and he didn't lie around in bed like she did.

I rode beside the train tracks and watched the sun glistening on them, and I would have been glistening too, if anyone cared to look. Sometimes you just have to be your own eyes. You have to see yourself shining and stop waiting for other eyes to see you.

The platform was empty. I lay down on the bench and waited, and for once I didn't care about waiting. I was spread over the bench with my red silk dress covering me, and the sun, fat like an egg yolk, glowing all over the day. It was dramatic in an absolutely quiet and private way. I was the hero reclining, as they do in paintings, with the blaze of silk and sun, spilled and flowing, giving me a glorious feeling, a kind of feeling that needed trumpets to accompany it. Soon a guard came, but he didn't play a trumpet. He just shuffled around and coughed.

chapter three

The train seemed to take a long time to arrive, and there was nothing to look at that I hadn't already worn out my observations on a million times before. There was the dim and empty platform opposite, and the bright channel of sky pouring slow morning light, leaving slabs of shadow on the ground. There was the air, creaking with the slight movement of trees leaning toward the sun. There was the flapping of birds, song spilling from their beaks and breaking over the leaves. There was probably even the dull thud of thoughts turning over inside heads sunk in pillows, and the patter of feet whose soft, slippered steps padded people up hallways toward the beginning of another day. Another day, I thought to myself and sighed because it was a hefty thought and I'd had to heave it out of myself, as if it bore the weight of all those people who wouldn't bother to think such a useless thought themselves.

But you had to face it; the days did just keep arriving, even if you didn't want them to. You had to get through them in one way or another: plod up the hall, spread some butter on toast, and go. "Not this one, though," I told myself. I'd decided it would be different. I wasn't plodding, I was swooping and carousing, and though everything else seemed just waking, my thoughts were already busy hopping from one thing to another, like a sparrow on a lawn.

I was still thinking about Harry, actually, even though he was exactly who I didn't want to be thinking about. I meant to tell him, before I left, that I didn't hold him responsible for what happened. I never said I did, but he might have felt I did, by the way I acted around him afterward. Like a cold fish. I didn't *feel* like a cold fish. I just didn't feel like anything I'd ever felt like before. And there were expectations. People were looking at me as if I was an exhibit. Exhibit B, Miss Disaster Study. So I was taking great care to hold everything inside. I was all buttoned up and private. I didn't know what kind of monstrous thing might come out if I let it. So I shut up and became cold stiff fish numero uno.

The very first time I saw Harry he didn't strike me as being anything in particular, but he did have an effect. I was looking straight at him, but he didn't notice me at all. He didn't even give me a look. Most boys give a girl at least a look, but Harry Jacob didn't. He was lifting an old church pew into his house. He had it on his shoulder and he was humming or whistling, and he looked as if he was having a nice time just lifting that pew into the house. He seemed more interested in how to angle the thing through the door than in having a squiz at someone else. I wasn't looking because I fancied him or anything, but just to see what kind of a family was moving into that

holding yourself in.

old mint-chew house. I was betting they'd be bogans or animal abusers, but they weren't. They were the Jacobs, and Harry was the youngest. Still, he was older than me, and he could drive.

Driving impressed a lot of girls, but not me. Susie Newbound only went with guys who drove. If he could take her to Bendigo and buy her a Big Mac, then he was the man for her. She wasn't fussy. I was. I was very particular. It wasn't that I had tickets on myself, it was just that I didn't feel anything for most of the boys at our school. I don't know why. Maybe I was hard of feeling. But I was waiting for the real thing, for someone first-class.

I spent a lot of my life waiting, to tell you the truth, which was why I was getting out of town. It was a deliberate strategy, a counter-attack to waiting, which wasn't getting me anywhere. There are two types of waiting. There's the waiting you do for something you know is coming, sooner or later — like waiting for the 6:28 train, or the school bus, or a party where a certain handsome boy might be. And then there's the waiting for something you don't know is coming. You don't even know what it is exactly, but you're hoping for it. You're imagining it and living your life for it. That's the kind of waiting that makes a fist in your heart.

When I was as small as a dog, I went and lay down on the couch and spread my hair out, the way Sleeping Beauty would've spread her hair. I closed my eyes and smiled, just the way an angel would smile if it had accidentally fallen asleep on a couch. I waited with my sleeping hair and my angel smile for Mum to come looking for me. But she never came looking. She never came and found me like that. Usually, after about a minute, I got sick of lying still. Or Eddie would burst into the room with a water pistol and ruin the atmosphere. I was used to Eddie ruining atmospheres. He really knew how to do that. I don't know if it was because he was older or because he was a boy, but Eddie always took up more room.

As I sat on the platform, the morning light was all broken up and gleaming, winking diamonds of it caught in the scraggly blue trees. Long shadows lay over the yellowed fields like leftover fingers of night still stroking the paddocks in sleep. But I wasn't one bit sleepy. I just couldn't find a strong line of thinking to follow, since Harry Jacob thoughts kept cutting into thoughts about Eddie, or about poor Dad, or the thing I most of all wanted to think about: the thing I didn't know yet, the thing that was like a runaway kite pulling my heart forward. That pulling forward thing was exactly what Harry didn't have. But I can't remember a time when there wasn't something tugging at me. My body was forever making plans, pushing awake all stupid and eager, a conspiracy of flesh and sap pulling me onward and onward. And I was just a hapless passenger, weary, bleary-eyed, sitting sideways, waiting to become the real Mannie — not the old Mannie, but the new one, the better one, the very best truest Mannie. It was as if the best truest Mannie lay miles ahead of me in the future and it was this Mannie Clarkeson who tugged me forward. That's why (I explained as if Harry was listening) I had to change tracks, not go up and down the same old roads. I wasn't getting closer to the best truest Mannie at Blackjack Road. I needed a new arc of sky to unwind the odd and faltering thread of my life into. I just did.

chapter four

By the time the train came there were quite a few people gathered on the platform. I stayed at the end near the bushes and planned not to bump into anyone I knew.

You should never plan.

On the train Alison Porrit's mother almost sat right next to me, but when she saw it was me she changed her mind.

"Oh, Manon," she said as if I wasn't a real person, as if I was a cow poo she'd accidentally trodden on. "Hello."

"Hello." I was sitting next to the window. She stood before me, clutching a snakeskin handbag and smiling.

"And what are you up to? So early?"

I didn't like seeing Mrs. Mrs. Porrit. In my mind I called her a double-Mrs. because that's what she was, more Mrs. than anything else, so I had no intention of telling her what I was up to. For a start, the way she asked made it sound as though I was involved in a World War Three conspiracy. Mrs. Mrs. Porrit always thought Eddie and Harry Jacob and I were bad influences on her Alison. So, Mrs. Mrs.

Porrit and I weren't off to a good start. I said I had business in Melbourne. She sniffed and put her hand to her mouth as if it was about to make an unseemly sound.

"You're very dressed up, Manon," she observed, raising her eyebrows in a way I didn't exactly appreciate.

"Yeah, I am." I agreed with her, but only on this one point. I even ran my hands over my dress and fussed about it a bit, just to emphasize my tremendous worthwhile elegance. Mrs. Mrs. Porrit's face became all long-nosed and pinched-up, like a goldfish who has suddenly come up against the glass. It quite amused me to think of Mrs. Mrs. Porrit as a goldfish, and I was compelled to watch her as she flapped her plump pink fins all the way to another seat. Then I pulled back the ugly plaid curtain and rammed my gaze up against the window.

I decided I'd just start again from here. Forget the Harry Jacob sighting and the bike ride and snotty Mrs. Mrs. Porrit. This was the real start of my new life. A train was a perfect place to start an adventure. Movies, for instance, always start at the platform in a cloud of mist, or dust, or something to blur the edges.

As my train pulled out of the station there was no mist, only a big dad in a red Windbreaker running along the platform, waving to his child. His tummy bumped up and down, but still he ran all the way to the end of the platform, puffing and waving. The few strands of hair that he had left on top of his head ruffled up so that he looked like an overused stuffed toy. I didn't like the feeling it was giving me, watching that big pale dad puffing and running and aching in his floppy old heart as the train pulled out with his little child. That child was probably on its small knees looking out and hooting with the joy of that chugging, shaking train and the way it seemed to take you through life, instead of life always passing by you.

A woman sat down opposite me. I was annoyed at her for sitting there. The moment of my departure was meant to be completely mine and I needed it to remain open and full of possibility, like a window without glass. So I felt as territorial as a barking dog about my moment, only I didn't bark. I used the more sinister strategy of neglecting to make the woman feel welcome. Not only that, I looked at her as if she were a dirty great cloud drifting into my endless clear sky. It didn't make her get up and flap away like Mrs. Mrs. Porrit, but she turned her head and looked out the window, and I consoled myself that my bad behavior had warded off potential discussions about her bright-spark children winning races and trophies and prominent positions. It would have really annoyed me if my unfriendliness, which was sour and sinking inside me, had been for nothing.

The woman wasn't what Eddie called a babe. She was about fifty, and had a pear-shaped head that made it look as if all the matter inside had sunk down into the jaw and filled it out too much. She wore a serious expression, and her lips were moving in a whispery way, as if there was a thought or word she was rolling over in her throat. She was dressed in dark, loose-fitting clothes, though she did have a large floppy white hat on her lap. She bent down and pulled a sandwich out of her bag, took half, and ate it carefully, cupping her hand underneath in case some of it fell. It didn't. It was a very well-packed sandwich, with grated carrot and other healthy things. A person who bothers to grate carrot for their sandwich is a very particular person, a person quite unlike me. I imagined her folding the corners of her blankets. I started thinking about all kinds of things she probably did that I never did: like dabbing her mouth with a napkin, or keeping all her socks matched, or taking an umbrella just in case, and doing up her seat belt every time. I pictured her at charitable dinners with a husband who was unspectacular but wore a necktie. I figured she had normal thoughts too, and she said kind things to her two children. And her two children would grow up with T-bar sandals and optimistic outlooks. What did her husband do? Real estate agent? I had no respect for real estate agents. Harry said I was judgmental. But Harry wasn't discriminating. He never was. He accepted anybody. Any old body.

The woman began peeling a mandarin. She put the skin in a brown paper bag, then broke the mandarin in half and leaned forward, with one half wobbling on her flat palm. She was offering it to me.

"No, thank you," I said. The words bolted out before I had time to think. I looked down immediately and saw the woman's shoes, which were alarming and not at all in keeping with the rest of her. I felt vexed by this. No one likes being contradicted by a pair of shoes. They were more like socks with rubber on the bottom and a special place for the big toe. And not only was she wearing funny shoes, she was offering me some mandarin. I looked up at her.

"Are you going to Melbourne?" I asked with a little world-weary sniff. The last thing I felt like was chatting. Some people are natural at chatting and they can talk to anyone. But I can't. People weren't likely to like me.

"Yep, well, kind of, straight to Tullamarine. I've got a flight to catch."

"Where to?"

"Just to Sydney." She smiled at me, as if she was a little bit amused, and I leaned forward.

"What are you doing in Sydney?" I asked, knowing it wasn't quite right to ask.

"I've got work to do there. I'm only going for the day."

"Do you live in Castlemaine?"

"I wish I did. I live in Melbourne. My parents live in Fryerstown. They've retired there. I was just visiting. What about you? Where are you going so early?"

I sat up straight and crossed my legs like a lady.

"To Melbourne. I've got some business there." I knew she was thinking I looked funny in a long red dress at six o'clock in the morning. I folded my arms across my chest.

"Business, huh?" She grinned as if she might even understand just how delicate a matter my business was. I considered explaining, but when I reached back into my mind I couldn't find the right beginning. It was the cold fish state of affairs. You can't go telling stuff when you're still swollen with it. I had to swallow it down first and make it regular, packageable, clean like a box. Something I could carry around without it causing a disturbance, without it causing floods or gaping.

I shifted in my seat and looked at the woman — right in her eyes — not to see her but just to hold on to something. Her eyes were soft, and I felt all right looking at her soft eyes.

She was actually quite different from what I'd first thought, now that I knew she wasn't a country person. To me, a person's interestingness was measured by the lines of distance that spanned from where I lived out into the world. The longer your line was, the better you became. Once I met a man who had been to Argentina. So far, he was the best.

"What's your business?" I asked the woman. She spat a pip into her hand.

"Theater director. And you?" She said it softly, as if she'd just said *dental nurse* or *bank teller*. I was suddenly ashamed of myself.

"Me, I don't do anything yet. I'm only seventeen. Are you really a theater director?"

"I'm afraid so." The woman shrugged apologetically.

"Well, my mum was an actress." I smacked my palms onto my knees in triumph.

"Really? What's her name? Maybe I know of her." She had a half smile on her face. It was secretive and inward, but it showed up in the open shape of her eyes. I let myself be encouraged by it.

"Emma. Emma Legrande. And then, when she married my dad, she was Emma Clarkeson. But you wouldn't know of her because she was an actress in France, before she came here. She didn't do any acting here."

"Why not?"

"She wasn't well. And she lived in the country. You can't do anything in the country." I rolled my eyes and shook my head to indicate the frustration that I myself was subject to, living in the country. The woman nodded, and I felt sure she understood. She was, after all, a theater director, and I had a lot of respect for those kinds of people, creative people like my mother.

"Well, I reckon you've inherited your mother's theatricality, anyway."

"How can you tell?" I said, resting my hand on my chest.

"Well, I guess I'm used to telling, part of the job. But the dress is a dead giveaway."

"Not as much as your shoes," I said with a little pout. At this the woman laughed out loud. She pulled her pants up a bit and lifted her feet to show them better. She faced the rubber soles toward me and explained that she got the shoes in Japan while she was working with a Butoh company, and that they were so comfortable that she forgot to take them off sometimes. I had no idea what a Butoh company was, but I didn't let on since the woman thought I was a theatrical person, and true theatrical people should know what Butoh was. So I said, "Of course," and "Once I almost wore my slippers to school too," which was true.

"I'm Helena."

"Manon." As I reached my hand toward hers I felt that I was doing something utterly perfect. Even the way I said my name — "Manon," not "I'm Manon," not "Mannie Clarkeson," just "Manon" — was exactly as it should be. Exquisite and delicate. Not too much one way or another, just hitting the right lovely ringing note. The quiet music of it surged through me and, just as the glow of the sun spread over the fields, I could have shone with it. I lifted my palms to my cheeks to touch the glow and, even after Helena took out a book and I sank into my seat and stared out the window, I could still feel the moment's perfection smoldering within me. The skinny old trees and bare pastures looked like they'd just put on a brand-new, luminous dress.

I knew it was a sign.

chapter five

The train arrived in Melbourne at eight o'clock in the morning. Helena gave me a card with her telephone number. *Helena Dubrovnic*, it said. I put it in my wallet. She said I could call her if I needed to. She smiled at me and I could tell that she was a true person, not like Mrs. Mrs. Porrit. She wasn't smiling for the sake of niceness, to make sure she got to heaven. I didn't know why she thought I'd need to ring her, though.

"Oh," I said, "I'll be visiting a relative."

She couldn't have known it was a lie because I said it very nice and prompt, as if it was the truth, as certain as a pale hand in a white glove extending out.

When Helena walked away, I almost wished I could go with her. I pictured her home for a minute. I thought it would have large couches and paintings on the walls, and maybe she would ask me to live with her forever and I would become a star protégée in her theater company, and we would eat in restaurants and laugh. But she hadn't asked me, so I couldn't. I went and got my bike.

The station was crammed with people who tunneled forward and backward with small cases banging at their knees. I weaved my bike through them and frowned, just to create a serious impression. In case people might think I looked funny in my red dress, I held myself quite like a member of Parliament and steered straight into the city, with purpose.

It wasn't pretend purpose. I did have important business. It was the kind of thing that only I could do. I couldn't explain it to anyone either, not even to Harry. It was a matter of the heart, a heart-knowing, anyway, that was telling me to do it.

I had this idea of going to a restaurant, first, to settle in. And not just any restaurant. I had a particular one in mind. My mum had taken Eddie and me there once when we were kids. She'd dressed up too for the occasion. We'd caught the train from Castlemaine. I remember she was wearing a long dark coat and a green silk scarf with white spots. She smelled lovely, and she had dark red lipstick, which she fixed up with a little round mirror that fitted in the palm of her hand. She wrote her name on the foggy train window and then she wrote Eddie, and then she wrote my name too, and she drew a heart shape around all the names, although my name went over the line a bit. She was happy. At the restaurant there was a man in a suit who bought me and Eddie some strawberry ice cream. It wasn't our dad, but we didn't care. Eddie and I played on the stools. It was a classy place. We had a good time there.

I thought that maybe I should be an actress too, like Mum. But I wasn't sure I had it in me. I didn't like people looking at me, whereas Mum liked it. She didn't only like it, she needed it. It was as if she was in darkness until people were looking at her, shining the light of their eyes upon her. Then she just lit up like our nice glass lamp shade with the roses on it. She got that glittery look. Her eyes opened wide and she would glide about and throw her head back and laugh, or sweep her hair in some way, making it bounce on her shoulders. Her light would fill a room. She'd make people want to keep looking at her. She'd be like a joker. She'd do anything, even put on funny voices. Then, once there was no one to see her, she switched off again, back into darkness. Her mouth sank down into a thin line, like a seam, and her eyes dulled like dry stones. Most of the time she would lie in bed.

I didn't really count for Mum, not as someone worth switching on for. Neither did my dad. Eddie did. And other people did; anyone she didn't really know counted, at first. She got tired of people quickly, though. She could use you up, all your eye power, especially if you weren't important or rich or educated. She would be nice at first, but once she knew you just a little, she didn't care anymore. You had no more charge; you were as useful as a dead old leaky battery. She had a thing about Eddie, though. It wasn't just that he was a male, because Dad was a male and that didn't work for him. It was because Eddie was like her. He was a natural. It was almost like loving herself, the way she loved Eddie.

Then there was the stinking hot summer that made things strange. That was when I first got an inkling about Harry Jacob, and when Susie Newbound got pregnant by Luke Nelson and had to go and live in Bendigo with him. But as far as Mum was concerned, that was the summer Eddie decided he wasn't going back to school.

When he said it at dinner, Mum went stiff and her eyes looked crazy. She turned to Dad and said, "Ned, he can't."

"Why not?" said Eddie.

Dad put down his fork and made a speech.

"You need a proper education. Believe me. One day you'll regret this. You may not think you need it now, but later you will. Finish your final year, then take time to think about what you want to do."

Before Eddie even had a chance to respond, Mum put her head in her hands and began to cry.

"See, Ned, see. It's because we live here. The types he's friends with. No one in the country is educated. This is your fault. You fix it. Tell him. Tell him what will become of him if he gets a trivial job here. He will amount to nothing. Oh, Eddie, you could be so good if you wanted." She turned finally to Eddie, reaching her hand to him. Eddie told her to calm down. But she didn't. That's when she hit on Harry Jacob as the cause.

"Is it Harry?" she cried. "Is it because he's left school?"

"Nuh. It's nothing to do with Harry. It's just I'm not interested in school." Eddie was getting uncomfortable. "Would you calm down,

Mum? It's not such a big deal." He folded his arms across his chest and looked away from her.

"It's Harry. I know it is. Eddie, he's a farmer's son. He doesn't have your ability. Ned!" She turned to Dad. "You have to stop this foolishness." She gripped the side of the table. "Eddie, I forbid you. I absolutely forbid you!"

"Jesus Christ!" Eddie snorted in disgust and got up from the table. Eddie and I were the same like that; we simply couldn't have people telling us what to do or what not to do. She should have known that. Dad leaned over to her.

"Emma —"

She lifted her hand and halted him. She closed her eyes and held everything still for a moment, like a conductor creating a silence in the piece. Then she left the table too. Dad sighed. It was a shame, because lately Mum had been better. There hadn't been a fight for quite a few weeks, and she'd been out of bed a lot and buying herself new clothes. She was even cooking meals. The funny thing was that in some ways she turned out to be right. It would have been better if Eddie hadn't hung around with Harry, but not for the reasons she said.

Dad came home one night clutching a bunch of red roses. He held them upside down by the stalks, with the flowers hanging by his knees. He looked frightened. He raised the roses slowly as if he wasn't sure he should.

She didn't smile. She narrowed her eyes and lifted her nose, and then she wiped her hands on a towel and snatched the roses from him. She threw them to the floor.

"You think you can just make everything all right with a bunch of flowers?" she shouted at him.

Eddie and I were sitting at the table eating cheese on toast. She wasn't eating, she was standing at the sink. Dad didn't speak.

"Well?" she demanded. He sighed and looked down at the flowers as if he was considering whether to pick them up or not.

"Emma," he said softly, and whatever he meant to say got caught up in his throat and it faltered and dissolved on his tongue as his mouth hung open and his hands rose toward her. She shook her head and stared at him with such a look of disgust that he turned away and left the room. I heard him walk down the hall, take his keys, and quietly shut the front door as he left the house. She ran to the hall and started to scream.

"You're useless," she called after him. "You're a nothing. You make me miserable. I wish I never —"

"Shut up, Mum," Eddie yelled. He sprang up from his chair and knocked over a glass of water. His eyes were flashing but he didn't say anything else; he just stood there. I picked up the glass.

Her hand was creeping up her neck and pressing at it. Her mouth was trembling and she took short breaths. Her face contorted, but she couldn't find the right expression. She was panicking. She wanted to shout at Eddie but she couldn't. For a second she gripped him with her mad eyes, but when Eddie looked away she fixed her gaze on the broken-up roses instead. Petals lay across the floor like some kind of injury. She glared at those poor busted roses as if they'd caused her an insufferable injustice, and since the roses didn't deny it she plunged toward the sink with a dramatic sigh and bent over it, sobbing. I put my hand on her back. She turned the taps on full blast and wouldn't look at me. Then she ran out of the room and threw herself on the bed. Through the whole house you could hear her sobbing.

"Fuck," said Eddie. "Fuck, I hate this." He was staring at the running water.

"Poor Dad." I turned off the taps.

"Fuck it," Eddie said, and he turned the television on so that it was louder than the sobbing.

It was Dad's softness that made Mum scream at him, just like how pillows make you want to punch them.

chapter six

I found that restaurant. I think it was the one. It had the right stools, anyway. It was at the top end of the city, on Bourke Street. There was a long bar on one side and a long bench against a wall on the other. The floor was checked and there were stools on poles stuck into the ground so you couldn't pull one closer to the other. People sat on either side, most of them hunched over newspapers, with one hand shoveling in food. No one seemed to notice me. No one bothered to look up from their newspapers, even though I was in the long red dress. I couldn't decide if that was good or bad; obviously I wasn't looking too shocking, but then I couldn't have been looking too damn captivating either. I figured if you balanced it up I came out looking middle-range, which was okay with me. So I leaned my elbows on the bar and considered the cakes, which appeared to be showing off and waiting there for me to decide.

The waiter was a thick grayish man, swollen with weariness and moving slowly, like a mollusk. He rubbed the inside of a glass with a tea towel and then, leaning back into the bench, called out in Italian to a short woman in the kitchen who was shaped like a dumpling and wore gold hoop earrings. She was bent over pots, wiping bowls, and sighing.

"Now, signorina?" he said, tucking the tea towel in his pants.

"I'll have that." I pointed to a yellow cheesy-looking cake.

"With cream?" He pulled a pencil out from behind his ear and wrote on a small pad.

"Can I have ice cream?"

"You can have whatever you like," he said, and smiled. It was true, no one was here to tell me not to.

While I waited, I stared up at a faded poster of kangaroos on a beach, above the shelves of oranges and wine bottles. Next to that was a painting of a stormy ocean, but neither of these stirred me, so I surreptitiously examined the patrons instead.

Next to me, at the bar, there was a man and a woman. I couldn't see the woman's face, since she was twisting toward the man. Her elbow leaned on the bar quite close to me and it was a very elegant bare, brown arm with a gold watch and a cigarette dangling between the fingers. Every now and then her hand disappeared from view and went to her mouth, but then it swung back to where I was, so that small curling trails of smoke floated into my face.

I didn't smoke, but right then it would have suited me to smoke. Well, it would have suited my red dress and the different feeling I had in it. Smoking looked like such a deliberate thing: considered and controlled, but finished off with the quiet murder of the little red ash and the pensive curl of smoke, aimless in the air like a dreamy afterthought, a final calm. I was lacking in deliberate qualities and final calms myself, so I watched the woman's hand as it pressed the butt into the white ashtray. I imagined it was my hand, being deliberate.

The man had his head tilted as if it had been struck by an obscurely angled thought that couldn't quite pass through into language. He didn't speak but the woman seemed anxious that he might. They were the kind of people you would expect to see in a classical, classy restaurant, and I felt a bit excited to be sitting next to them. Stylish-looking people, without dirty marks — the woman smelling of perfume and clean hair, and the man, I could tell, was a man who would never have dirt under his nails. If Harry could see me now, I thought. I wriggled on the seat and just when I was beginning to feel a little bit good about myself I got a glimpse of my sandals. Suddenly I knew they were all wrong. You can't wear sandals with a long red dress. The woman, for instance, was wearing shining black shoes with slender heels. I was giving myself away with those sandals. I was ruining the whole outfit. Anyone could tell. I hastily hid my clumpy worn old sandals under my dress and I felt my heart pound with the need for the right kind of shoes.

It wasn't an unusual way for my heart to be. Either curled up with the waiting or pounding with the wanting. That's two feelings that move all out of step with each other. Waiting doesn't really move, it doesn't have direction, whereas wanting dashes out of you, like an arrow. So if you wait and want and wait and want, then you live in a jagged way. You go along in zigzag, not in a clear line forward, like most people do. It's as if your bones stay put while your heart and soul bound so far forward you can't get them back. So maybe you're not even in one piece anymore, and you end up feeling desperate and grim like those poplars that lean, in an aching way, over the Nelsons' driveway.

Anyway, the first thing I ever really wanted was T-bar sandals. At school, girls wore them in summer with short socks. T-bars had holes shaped like clover in the top and a little buckle that did up like a belt. Mum said it was a waste of money to have one pair of shoes for summer and another pair for winter. I said I'd wear my T-bars all year-round, but she said, "Don't be silly, Manon. You can't wear sandals in winter."

So it was Mum's fault that I looked like a nerd in summer with my clunky lace-ups. First I tried cutting clover-shaped holes into them but they wouldn't cut, so I tried stabbing them with a barbecue skewer instead. It didn't work. I thought I could just punch out the right shapes, but I ended up with poky holes in my lace-ups, which made me look even worse than I already did. I could tell that people were looking at my shoes. They were all probably talking about it at school.

That's how Lucy Brixton became my best friend. Lucy was much taller than me, and her hair was milk white, thick, and dead straight.

It was always wound up in big plaited buns on top of her head so she looked old-fashioned and odd. Her mother did it for her. But at least Lucy had T-bars, and at least her mother didn't talk in a funny accent like mine. Then Lucy's T-bars broke at the buckle and her mum was going to chuck them out and buy Lucy a new pair, but I said I'd take the busted ones. Lucy gave them to me, just like that, and I fixed them up with a safety pin. I was happy as anything in those T-bars. I sat next to Lucy in class. She lived near Harcourt Station, so we went home together on the bus. For a while I felt just like any other normal kid at school. For about a week, actually. For one glorious week I couldn't stop gazing down at my T-bars. I so liked the way they made me seem right that I snuck looks all the time, especially when I needed an extra boost of confidence. Once, at lunchtime, I even walked up to a gang of eleventh graders, sat down next to Charlie Buttrose, and stretched my legs out and crossed my ankles over just so they could all see my T-bars. Charlie Buttrose was a golden-skinned god who didn't say anything to me, so after a while I went and found Lucy and we squashed figs into the concrete.

After that it started to fade, the T-bar effect, and slowly I returned to being just me again. It was worse than you would imagine, the fading of the T-bar effect, because it meant that all along I was wrong. All along I was thinking that if only I had T-bars I'd be like everyone else. But it wasn't the case. It wasn't the lack of T-bars that was making me like I was, it was something else. And that meant I had to keep looking.

The only thing I knew was that whatever I wanted, I wanted it badly.

Anyway.

I looked at the man, who was almost facing me, though the woman was between us. He was scratching his chin and frowning. His hair was short and the color of charcoal, and he was wearing cuff links. He pulled his shirtsleeve up to look at his watch. The woman sighed and complained about the heat, about how it made her panic, but the man appeared to have lost interest. He lifted his eyes over the woman's shoulder and he looked at me as if he knew that I was listening. I quickly turned to the faded kangaroo poster. But after a moment I looked back and there he was, staring straight at me. It wasn't an indignant stare, it wasn't even curious. It was a stare I was meant to see. He shot it right at me. I turned away and I didn't look back again.

chapter seven

Eddie and I once saw a pervert. I was only thirteen when we saw him. We were waiting at the bus stop, which was an annoying place, and things always went funny when you just had to stand and wait by the road. Especially for me since, as I said, it didn't suit me to wait. The shelter there had a pebble-mix surface and brown concrete edges. It was ugly as hell and you had to resent it a bit. We never sat under the shelter, we sat on the wall nearby, or we just stood and leaned. If Eddie was in the mood, we did things, like throw stones at the Give Way sign.

This time Eddie wasn't in the mood, so I just had my foot up against the wall. I was kicking myself in and out from the wall — in and out, in and out — making a rhythm in my head. A car pulled up and a man leaned over and curled his finger toward me, motioning for me to come over. Eddie was just leaning and thinking and he didn't seem interested, so I kicked myself out from the wall and went over to the car. The man looked a bit like Mr. Tony from the milk bar: dark and bleary-eyed, with a well-pressed, lemon-colored shirt. I remember that as I stuck my face up to the window I was hit by an odor that wasn't exactly roses. Maybe it was only an ugly mix of old sweat and smoke, but it was still enough to make me take a fast step back. You can depend on your nose like that. My nose knew before I did that he wasn't a hero. He asked me if I knew where the Midland Highway was. Of course I did. Everyone did. It wasn't far away. I was half pointing and half talking to the man before I sensed again that something wasn't quite right. I stopped talking and had a proper look.

The man was holding his dick in his hand. His fly was undone and the thing was sticking straight up. I hadn't noticed at first, because he had pants on and only the end part was showing. It was pale like a knuckle when you make a fist. I eyeballed Eddie and he came over, pushed his way in front of me and looked in the window. Eddie was staring. So I looked again over his shoulder, just to make sure it really was what I thought it was. I knew I wasn't meant to look, but the man was looking at it too. We were all looking at it, as if it were a hurt animal. He must have been squeezing it.

Eddie said, "Whaddya want?" The man said he was looking for the Midland Highway and could we get in and show him and then he would take us home. He must have thought we were stupid. Even at that age I knew you shouldn't get in a car with a man, and especially not one who was disgusting. Eddie shook his head and told the man to get lost. The bus was coming then, so the man drove away. Eddie started to piss himself laughing and I did too, since it was exciting to have such a disgusting thing happen.

"Did you see? He was flogging it!"

"He's a pervert."

"We should've got the license plate."

"He could be a rapist."

"Yeah, as if we'd get in the car. That guy didn't have a chance in hell."

Eddie always had to tell things first. He was the oldest.

Mum was in bed when we got home. She wasn't really in bed this time. She was just lying on top of it, but still she wasn't dressed like a normal mum would be. She was in one of those adult nighties made of satin or silk, pearly and smooth like the inside of a shell, and edged in lace. It was skimpy, in an elegant way. She didn't look like a girl in a boarding school. You had to wonder why she bothered wearing such a nice-looking nightie when there was no one to see it anyway. She was fiddling with her hair and reading a magazine.

Eddie ran in and stood by the bed. I just hung in the doorway.

"We saw a pervert," said Eddie.

"What do you mean?" She let the magazine close and reached up to push Eddie's hair away from his face. She was gazing up at him as if he were a beautiful sunset.

"He had his dick out," I said. I stretched up to the top of the doorway and made myself extra long.

"Now, Manon . . ." Mum frowned as if she was about to get mad at me for saying "dick," but then her attention dissolved and she looked away.

"He did. It's true. He asked us to get in the car," said Eddie and he turned back to me, urgently, since he knew he needed my help to keep Mum interested. But I didn't care to help anymore. So Eddie dropped his schoolbag, just for the *bang* it made. Mum looked back at him and patted the bed.

"Tell me what happened."

Mum took us to the police station. We went into a room with the policeman. I remember he was wearing a cap and I was watching him writing down our answers, thinking that he wasn't writing very well and feeling concerned that a man in such a position, a position of authority, wasn't a good speller.

"What kind of car was it?"

"A white Holden," said Eddie.

"No, it wasn't, it was gray." I knew more about colors than Eddie. He might have been the natural but at least I was artistic — the art teacher said I was — I knew the color. Besides, I was the one who saw the car, not Eddie. But he always had to tell things first. The policeman smiled and glanced up at Mum, who crossed her legs over and swept her hair behind her ear.

"I don't s'pose you saw the license plate then, did you?"

"No," I said.

Eddie was squeezing his face and saying "Umm" as if he was try-ing to remember. Then he just said a number. I knew he was making it up because he didn't want to look stupid for not getting it in the first place. The policeman wrote down the number that Eddie made up. Now they'd never find that pervert, I thought.

"And you said the car was white?" he asked Eddie.

"Yep."

"Edouard would know," said our mother, and she put her hand on Eddie's leg and smiled, and you could tell the policeman liked her because he looked at her that way, as if it was a private look.

Later, Eddie and I told Dad about the pervert. We were laughing in the telly room. Mum got out of bed and stood in the doorway. Dad looked up at her.

"What's wrong, Emma?" he said. "You look like you've just seen a ghost." She stood there in such an accusatory way that we had to look at her. Her mouth was all bitten inward. Her feet peeped out the bot-tom of her dressing gown. Dad got up from the couch and walked toward her. She waved him away and pulled the gown together at her chest.

"I'm not going to sit on that couch. I just can't support it. It's revolting." She said "support it" when she meant she couldn't "stand it," because sometimes she got French words stuck in place of the right words. That annoyed me, because no matter how many times you told her how it should be, she still got it wrong. She did it on purpose to get more attention.

"What's wrong with the couch?" said Eddie, and we all stared at the poor old couch. We'd had it for as long as I could remember. It probably belonged to our grandparents, Ivy and Benjamin, in its glory days. You had to admit that it wasn't so glorious now. It had shiny curly gold patterns on it, and frayed arms, and holes in the cushions with a spring sticking out that was liable to tear your clothes if you didn't look out. There was an old brown wool blanket draped over to hide the holes, but it always fell down in a lazy wrinkle in the middle. The blanket was covered in dog hair.

"It makes me depressed. Every time I look at it I feel depressed," she declared, lifting her chin and looking down at the couch as if it was almost too ugly to even look at, as if she could only just bear to gesture toward it with her wavering fingers.

Dad sat on the edge of the couch and clasped his hands together.

"It's worn out," she cried. "Can't you see? It's worn out. It's rubbish." Her voice rose urgently and she aimed it at Dad, as if he'd done a terrible, terrible thing by making her live with a piece of rubbish. It made me wonder if indeed it was a terrible thing to be sitting on a piece of rubbish, though I'd never even seen it like that before. I stuck my finger under the threadbare bit on the arm and pulled the thread hard to see if it would break. Dad was looking up at her with his soft eyes. Eddie switched on the telly.

"We'll get it reupholstered then, shall we, Emma?" he said, cooing a bit like a pigeon does. She didn't reply. Her hands combed at her hair frantically.

"Don't worry about it tonight," he said. "Tomorrow you can telephone Mr. Bondarelli. Why don't you sit down?" He pushed Mou off the couch beside him and we made room for Mum. But she vanished, her bare feet pattering up the hallway. She went to her bedroom, and Mou climbed back on the couch.

chapter eight

This was my plan: There were two places I had to go to for my business, and after that I was leaving town. I was going to Paris, actually. The one benefit of having a French mother was that it entitled me to a French passport. Mum was always so precious about Frenchness, as if it made her special. Because of her, Eddie and I, and even Mou, which is short for *mouton* and means *sheep*, had had to put up with la-dee-da French names that didn't work here and just got shortened so they sounded like anyone else's name. In my mind, France would be a precious country where people would say my name in a la-dee-da way and it wouldn't sound out of place. And Paris was the most beautiful city in the world. We had a book about it at home, full-color pictures, Eiffel Tower, avenues of triumph, you know. Mum said it was the city of love. I was sure I was a lover, so where better than the city of love?

The horse money came from Nora, a nice lady, skinny as a piece of paper, with teeth that looked like corn. She was mad about horses and paid ten dollars a week to keep Buddy and Misty in our paddocks. I loved Buddy and Misty anyway, especially their velvet noses, so I would have paid to have them there. But Nora left the ten dollars in an envelope under the door if we weren't home. Whoever found it put it in the pot on the mantelpiece, above the wood stove. When it was full, Dad and Eddie planned to buy a ride-on mower. But that wasn't going to happen anymore, so I took it; I took seventy dollars and left the rest. I didn't expect it to get me to Paris. I had another idea about where that money was coming from.

The first place I was going to was Cyril Jewell House, Hope Street, Brunswick. It sounded like a house of jokers. I'd never been there before, but I'd always pictured it as a big red house on a windy hill, with turrets and spires and mysterious faces at the windows, and hand-knit jumpers flapping on the line. It was where my grandmother Ivy lived.

I figured I'd catch the train to Brunswick and ride my bike from there. I headed toward the center of the city and accidentally stopped at a shop called Shoe Biz. Dumb name for a shop, I thought, but the front window was enticing: shoes standing on shelves, getting ready. I was just having a vague old squiz, thinking about the importance or not of shoes (if you counted it against the other importances in your life), when a shop lady pounced on me. She was a splendid pouncer and was completely polished, with her hair pulled back so tight that her face was stretched into a permanent smile, and her skin so covered in thick face makeup that I couldn't have said what she was like underneath. She wore a tag that said DEBORAH, and her eyes were like small wet fidgeting pebbles that couldn't be covered up. I imagined she was a retired ballerina who liked cats and never stuck her finger in the jam. Who knows? I bet she had a Mason Pearson hairbrush, just like Lucy Brixton.

Anyway, Deborah admired my dress, so she got me inside and then led me around, darting like a hungry bird at the shoes she was sure I would like. I felt like a faker, actually, as if I was an obvious B-type person who was trying to buy an A-person disguise, trying to pretend I was a person with taste and money and style. You can't buy that kind of thing. Everyone knows that shoes don't make you any different. You can't move up in the world because your shoes are mighty. Deborah would have known that too, but it was her job to pretend otherwise.

Still, it was worth a try. I came out with a pair off the sale rack. They were slightly too big but half the price of the others. They were silver, though, with thin crisscrossing straps across the top. I put them straight on and walked down Bourke Street, listening to the way they went *clip clap* on the footpath. My toes poked out in a pretty good way. Sun was streaming down, and since the morning rush had already pummeled the streets they seemed momentarily emptied and calm, as if the city were taking a deep breath in the early morning lull. The few people left were sitting with bags on their laps and faces tilted to the sun, or standing at shop windows and considering, or waiting at tram stops with unfolded newspapers in their hands.

There were other bike riders lounging on the steps, but they were definitely authentic A-type bike riders since they had special bike clothes with helmets and clinging shorts. I wasn't going to ride past them in case they remarked to each other how stupid it was to ride a bike in a long red dress, so I walked, with my head unnaturally still, banking on them noticing instead what spectacular silver shoes I was wearing. Actually those silver shoes were beginning to make my back hurt, and that worried me as I didn't want my limp to get worse, not even for the sake of those shoes.

As I made my way to the station, I was thinking about that Shoe Biz shop lady, Deborah. She was probably only a couple of years older than me, but she made herself look old on purpose. Not old in a wrinkled way, old in a snappy handbag kind of a way. She was what Lucy Brixton wanted to become. Lucy even had a dressing table in her room, with a velvet stool shaped like a mushroom. That was where her pink Mason Pearson hairbrush lay, waiting for morning when Lucy's mum came in and brushed Lucy's hair, and plaited it and put elastic bands and bobby pins in it. Once, when I stayed the night, Lucy's mum offered to do my hair, but I was too embarrassed because I thought I might have knots, and my hair is donkey brown even though I wished it was milky. To tell you the truth, I didn't even know a Mason Pearson hairbrush was a special thing until Lucy told me. I couldn't imagine my mum doing my hair. Mostly my mum was asleep in the morning. Lucy's mum even made us lunch in a lunch box. I was so proud of having a proper lunch. Usually I mooched off big Betty Edmunds, who was always on a diet and would sometimes palm off her peanut butter sandwiches. When I got home I told Eddie about getting a proper lunch. I said I was going to ask for a Mason Pearson hairbrush for my birthday and Eddie scoffed. He said it was a stupid thing to ask for.

"You never even brush your hair, Mannie. Why don't you ask for a bike? That's what you really want."

"As if. As if they'd get me a bike."

"Yeah, but you can still ask for it. You never know," said Eddie.

I didn't get either. I got a book about a horse, called *National Velvet.*

After I saw Lucy Brixton's room, I fantasized about having one all to myself. I was particularly good at the art of fantasizing, probably due to my overactive imagination, but it was hard to pretend our room was elegant in any way. Eddie and I shared it, and it was hardly even a proper room. It was once just a veranda, but now it had walls and a window that looked over the paddock. You didn't get a clear view because there was a scruffy old melaleuca tree right in the way. The dark wooden ceiling sloped downward and the skirting board was missing, so there was a big gap where the wall met the floor. You could see the ground underneath the house, which is exciting when you're about six years old but a bit grim when you're seventeen. There was lino on the floor and underneath the lino you could find old newspapers, which Eddie sometimes read out when we were going to sleep. We had a bunk bed. I slept on the bottom and tried to bug Eddie by pressing my feet into his mattress, making moving mountains between the wood slats. There was a bulky, bursting, slack-jawed cupboard, a yellow bookshelf, a record player that was once Ivy and Benjamin's, and the five records that we'd gotten as birthday presents. It was nothing like Lucy's bedroom, where everything was white, matching, and seamless. She had two beds in it even though there was only one of her, but best of all it was never cold in Lucy's room. She had heater vents in the floor and you could sit around in your nightie. Eddie rolled up a blanket and stuck it in the gap in our room to stop the draft, but it didn't work properly. We sometimes slept in our wool hats.

Dad had to go to work very early, when we were still in bed. He'd come in and wake us, just to say good-bye.

"Dad, do you have to wake us up?" Eddie whinged.

"How else do I say good-bye?" he said. He gave us a kiss and then left. He did it every time, and after he left Eddie grumbled, but I didn't. I liked being woken up by Dad. I liked being woken in exactly that way. Eddie said I was a baby.

"Anyway, why do you have to say good-bye to him when you're just gonna see him again when he comes home?" said Eddie.

"I dunno," I said. "It's nice to say good-bye." What I liked was that it was a sure thing. It was regular; it was something I knew would happen, and it did happen, and I liked that. It was like one plus one equals two.

"You're acting tough, Eddie," I said, but he'd already gone back to sleep. Eddie didn't need to count on things like I did, because he was more normal than I was. He didn't even have a limp, for a start.

Sometimes I blamed Eddie, or the bus stop, or even that old woman for me getting the limp. I hadn't reached a final decision about which of them was really to blame, since it was easier to keep switching the blame between all three and never having to know who to be most angry at. Usually it was the old lady, who was a sticky beak, know-all, preachy type of old lady. Because I never saw her again, I could have furious imaginary conversations with her.

Eddie made up the game while we were waiting for that old school bus. The idea was to jump from the brick wall, catch hold of the top of the bus shelter, and swing from it. When Eddie did it, it looked easy. He was longer than me and he had more jumping power. But I was good at jumping too. The jumping part wasn't what went wrong. I climbed up on the wall and figured the distance was not more than a big puddle, and I'd jumped many of them before. The height was the scary part.

The old woman was standing hunched over a grocery cart, and when she saw me climbing the wall, she twisted her head backward and forward, and her mouth crinkled up in a sneer and she creaked out a warning.

"You stupid girl. You'll hurt yourself doing that. I'm telling you."

There was something about the old lady that made me feel mad. I frowned and puffed a breath out, almost a snort but not quite. In my heart I felt twitchy. I had to show that old lady, just show her. I was good enough to do anything Eddie could do. What would that old lady know?

So I jumped. My hands grabbed the top edge of the shelter but my legs flew out in front of me, with such a swing that they pulled my hands off and there was no chance of swinging my legs back. I landed on the pavement. My bum hit it hard. My head felt like it was thrown off, and a pain shot right up my spine and burned onto the backs of my eyes. But I got up straightaway and sat down neatly on the seat, and I said out loud, so that horrible old lady could hear me, "It didn't hurt." I was ashamed of myself — not for falling, but for being wrong.

Eddie knew. It did hurt. But he didn't say anything because if someone asks if you're okay that's what makes you cry. You can hold it in as long as no one gives you somewhere to pour it into. So Eddie just looked up at the shelter with his hands in his pockets. He said I would have made it, but the edge was too fat for my hands and they couldn't get a proper grip.

I didn't care about technicalities. I only cared that that old lady was right and I was wrong, and we both knew it, but I was the one who was hurting. And then I was worrying about my bones, the ones in the spine, especially at the bottom where there was a horrible pain. But I had to concentrate on not letting on about it, not giving that hateful old lady any more satisfaction. I tried wishing that the old lady would just crumble up like a stale old biscuit, but what really kept coming into my mind was the possibility that there was a big crack in my bones, and when I stood up they might just break.

But that didn't happen. I got on the bus and I told Eddie.

"I think I've done something. It hurts."

"Where?"

"Here." I showed him. "And I've got a headache too."

"That's the whiplash," he said. Then he frowned. He took my hand and pressed his thumb into it. He said that he'd heard it helped with headache. But it didn't. He said he'd get me one of Mum's pain-killers when we got home.

"You're not going to tell her, are you?" he said.

"No way. She'll just get mad at me. She'll say it was my own fault and I'm a stupid girl."

Eddie nodded, because he knew I was right.

When I started to limp because of the pain down my leg, Dad took me to see Dr. Roland. Dr. Roland had large sad eyes, and photos of his little girl stuck up on the wall. Dr. Roland said I had a disk injury with damage to the sciatic nerve, and I should lie on my back for six weeks.

"Six weeks?" I said. "No school for six weeks?"

"I'm afraid not," said Dr. Roland.

That was when it was good. For a moment it was unbelievably good. No school. No Math. No Latin. Mum even let me watch Ivan's Midday Movie Classic on telly, with a glass of lemonade. I lay out flat on the newly reupholstered couch. It was now a cherry color, with extra sleeves on the arm, and Mou wasn't allowed on it at all. After one day of lying out flat I was sick of it, and I started feeling bad about it, and then mad about it, and then I wanted to get cross at someone.

By the time one week was up and I still had five to go, I was beset by a big woe-is-me kind of a mood and couldn't summon any nice feelings for anyone else at all, especially since no one in the world was suffering like I was. And when Lucy came to visit and tell me what so-and-so said, and how so-and-so was smoking behind the penguin rubbish bin, and how they all went swimming down at Vaughan Springs and big Biff Lostren was wearing Speedos and everyone was laughing at him for wearing Speedos (because most guys wore boardies unless they came from Sydney), and so on, all I could do was sniff and squeeze out some stiff fake smiles.

"What have you been doing, Mannie?" asked Lucy, pulling her fingers through her ponytail.

"Nothing." I felt my face looking as sour as a dried-up lemon half.

During that unbearable six weeks, a man named Travis Houghton moved onto our land. He lived in a caravan, and he was an Odd

Jobs Man. He wore undershirts, and his arms were brown and chunky and looked like they were about to burst. He had golden wavy hair. He came inside our house sometimes to pay the rent, and Mum made him a cup of tea. He leaned back on the kitchen chair, put his arms behind his head, and said to me, "How's the little wounded bird?" I didn't like the way he spread himself out in that kitchen chair, as if he was very comfortable and had forgotten he was in somebody else's house. As if he wanted to make sure we could see as much of him as possible. He lifted his arms behind his head and leaned back on the kitchen chair and Mum didn't tell him off. At least whenever he was around, Mum would be nice. She gave Travis some biscuits for his tea and put the milk in a little green jug. Travis had a very deep voice. He asked Mum if she liked swimming and Mum laughed at him.

It wasn't just that those six weeks were such a killer, it was the overall effect of those six weeks. For one thing, my leg was never the same, and since my leg was never the same again, neither was I. After all, your leg is a major part of you, when you think about it. You don't feel right when even a little part of you, like, say, a baby finger, is a bit broken down. You feel limited. I felt as if I was stuck in a race and one leg wouldn't run. And running was more important to me than to most people. It really was. I liked movement. It made me feel great when I moved. Sometimes it could come over me all of a sudden, not suddenly wanting to move, but as if something was inviting me to move, something like a spaciousness in front of me, an empty stretch of land without an end. In fact, it was the endlessness which got me. I ran at it to test infinity, to become boundless, like an animal.

But I couldn't do that anymore. I was limited. It was as if a fence had grown up around me. It wasn't that I limped, it was just that I knew if I did wild things, like run or jump, I'd have a bad ache in my leg. Actually, I couldn't even sit down for a long time without the ache starting. So, I was truly damaged and I wasn't happy. I lost that feeling you have when you're a pure little kid, the feeling that you can do anything you want: You can do ten cartwheels in a row, you can become a champion. I knew I'd never be a champion. That's a lot to know when you're only fourteen.

chapter nine

Other people knew it too. Even with my T-bars, I could tell that people knew I wasn't going to be a champion. When I got back to school, Lucy Brixton had a new best friend. Lucy never actually said it, but I could tell I'd been replaced since she nearly always sat next to Kate Dolson and not me. In History I even ended up sitting next to Sharon Baker, the girl no one liked to sit next to because she had scaly hands and an irritating voice.

And when Sharon tried to get chummy with me, I knew it was a bad sign. Sharon was assuming that I'd become like her. She was relating to my skew-whiffness. She meant to make me an ally, a companion loser: her with her scaly hands and me with my bad-leg feelings. The loser club.

"I'll tell you something," said Sharon. She was recruiting, so I didn't listen. I could see Lucy and Kate, passing notes back and forth. Lucy had her milk hair all plaited up on top of her head like a Dutch milkmaid. Elaborate as always. She had white skin and little fat hands that pushed notes across the table. Lucy looked silly with her hair like that. She wasn't a Dutch milkmaid so why should she wear a Dutch milkmaid hairdo? It was putting on airs. That's what I thought, and I admit it was a bitter old thought. It was the creaminess in Lucy's nature. Maybe it didn't suit me anymore. Maybe scaly hands were okay. Lucy was giggling, her shoulders crumpling inward and a little dainty wisp of hair floating at her neck. I didn't like that little wisp. I hated it, in fact.

"Jeez, Manon. Did ya hear what I said?" said Sharon. "You wanna piece of chewie or don't ya? It's Wrigley." I didn't want Sharon to pass me anything right then, not even a chewie. Scaly hands weren't okay. Everyone knew Sharon had eczema and you could catch it if you touched her hands. I slumped my head on my elbows and turned away. And then I just closed my eyes and I listened to myself breathing.

It wasn't that Lucy was mean. She was still friendly to me. It was more that I didn't believe in me as much as I did before. I wasn't sure who I was, so I was awkward and halting. I knew I was behaving like a loser, but I couldn't stop it. Lucy came over to my house, but I had a feeling she was coming over for something else, not to see me. Even in the best of times I felt anxious when anyone came over, because of my mum, because you could never tell how she would be. We were playing Eddie's Clash records in the living room.

"How come your house is so messy?" said Lucy, who was sitting on the newly reupholstered couch. It was Lucy who wanted to hear Eddie's records. (I was sick of The Clash myself.)

"I dunno. 'Cause of my mum; she gets headaches. She can't clean up 'cause she has headaches." It wasn't quite a lie. Sometimes Mum said she had a headache, and that was why she was in bed. But I didn't really understand what was wrong with her. I just knew that you couldn't count on her to be anything. She was always in a mood, she never just was; never just a plain clear sky, always weather changes slipping and rippling across her face. So we were on alert all the time. If Eddie got home after me, he'd come and ask me how she was. It was easier if you were prepared, especially if the weather was storm cloud, because then you could just piss off for a while, over to the Jacobs' or to the Hills' to watch *Bewitched* on telly.

"Anyway, she's good looking, your mum," pronounced Lucy, as if it was a compensation.

"So they say." I flicked through the records.

"My dad says your mother's a beautiful woman, even if she is schizo."

"Schizo?" I squinted at Lucy. Pretty was one thing, but schizo was another.

"Where's Eddie?" she said, standing up and looking out the window.

"How should I know?"

Lucy was looking at the bungalow. Eddie had moved out of our bedroom because he said he needed his own room. I was right. Lucy hadn't come over to listen to records with me. Eddie was the real reason for her visit. Girls at school were always asking me questions about him. They even rang him up.

61

chapter ten

I got to Flinders Street Station, but I didn't exactly feel like going in. It looked like a dirty gaping mouth with too many words coming in and out of it, and I felt weary at the thought of being buffeted by an argument of people. There was a skinny guy sitting on the steps playing guitar and singing in this quiet frail voice, his face looking up like a hungry bird. He seemed aimless, like a shepherd, and had a prominent and eager lifting nose and grubby red sneakers. I dropped some horse money in his guitar case. I was glad he was there. I don't know why. Because he wasn't going in or out. Because he was just there.

Harry Jacob played guitar, but not in a frail-bird way. That was why Eddie made friends with him. Eddie couldn't concentrate long enough on anything to be able to learn to play the guitar. He was only good at things that came naturally to him, things he didn't have to work at, like footy and cricket and waltzing and laughing and girls. Everything else, like schoolwork, he didn't care about. Harry didn't even play footy. Straightaway that made Harry Jacob odd. If you were a boy who didn't play footy, people were liable to call you a pansy. But Harry got away with it because he was tall, because he played guitar, and because he was Eddie's mate and Eddie was captain of the local side. Eddie never told us he was captain; we read it in the local newspaper.

Harry had a big family and he was the youngest. The Jacobs were once farmers but their dad had gone into real estate, since there was a drought and farming was "bad on the back." Harry's family didn't put any pressure on Harry; he wasn't expected to be anything.

Harry and Eddie got along easily, probably because Harry wasn't in awe of Eddie. And probably because Eddie had a lot of respect for the things that he didn't have, and they were exactly what Harry had. Harry knew where he was. Eddie didn't know a thing about what he wanted. In fact, I reckon that instead of wanting to get something, Eddie wanted to lose something. You had the feeling that he wanted to just shake it off, like a dog shakes off water after a swim. Only it couldn't be shaken off, so instead he didn't let it settle. Eddie never settled. You couldn't tie him down to anything. He never made promises. It drove girls crazy. Eddie never promised a girl anything.

A lot of action started to go on around then. And I mean that kind of action. For example, Susie Newbound came to school and let loose that Barry Hill had kissed her boobs. Susie was tall and she had big ones. She didn't tell everyone. She just told Ellen Green, and Ellen told Sharon Baker, and Sharon, who never gave up on befriending me, told me.

"You're kidding? On the skin?" I said. I was only fourteen and a slow developer in that area. I didn't understand how a kiss like that could be anything but humiliating.

"Yep. On the skin. Apparently she didn't care." Sharon, who was delivering the scoop to me, wriggled her body in a mock shiver. We shivered together in a repulsed way.

I wasn't really repulsed; I was alarmed. Did that happen to Susie because she had big ones, or would that happen to everyone? Even me? And if it happened to me, how the hell would I not die of embarrassment? I didn't even want to be looked at, let alone kissed, and certainly not on such private parts. I comforted myself with the observation that Susie Newbound's boobs stuck out and made you notice them, like you'd notice a speed bump in the road if you were riding your bike. The rest of Susie didn't stick out; it wasn't unusual or uncoverable. She had freckles and a small head and she straightened her hair.

I told Lucy. "Guess what? Susie Newbound got her boobs kissed."

Lucy rolled her eyes. "I know," she hissed. "Philomena's been doing it with Froggo." She muffled her triumph with a casual shrug. But I saw it. I saw her enjoying knowing more than me, knowing a better, saucier thing.

"Philomena?" I was incredulous. Philomena, that sour old rectangle who never liked me. "And Froggo?" Froggo worked at the gas station. He was okay. He used to have pimples, but not anymore.

"Yep. They've been doing it for ages. The whole way."

"How do you know?"

"I just heard."

If it was true, that would make Philomena the first person I knew who had actually done it. Sometimes it came into my mind, Philomena and Froggo doing it. At that stage, I didn't know what "it" would look like, but whenever I saw Philomena on her bike, avoiding me, I got a nasty picture of her and fat Froggo making movements. I didn't want to think about it. But sometimes it's as if there's a movie playing inside your head and you're not even the operator. It just went to show, I thought. And then since I wasn't sure what it showed, I just notched the fact down in my mind as an important indicator of the mysterious unknowable order of things. It was never as you'd expect. Still, I challenged Lucy. I said it couldn't be true. Lucy didn't say anything. She shrugged again, acting unimpressionable. She always did that. Lucy and I weren't best friends anymore. We were just so-so friends.

I was sixteen and still hadn't had a proper boyfriend by the time that deadly hot summer arrived and the bad things were beginning. It was as if life's brain went balmy and mean after that summer, as if it had bad sunstroke. For starters, there wasn't enough flowering and nectar in the bush, so the birds were compelled to eat Mr. Nelson's Pink Ladies. Mr. Nelson called them the pariahs of the sky; he acted as if the poor birds were criminals. He grew red and fat and desperate, and sometimes got up at dawn with Mrs. Nelson and they stood at the edge of their orchards on little yellow steel ladders, clapping at the parrots and finches who scampered across the sky looking for Pink Lady apples.

That was the summer Susie Newbound got pregnant, and Eddie dropped out of school. It was the same summer that Ruth Warlock went missing. I didn't know Ruth Warlock very well, since she was only a little kid, but I saw her picture in the papers and everyone talked about her all the time. She was only seven, and everyone said she was too young to be going to school on her own. In the newspaper picture she looked like such a regular gap-toothed happy girl, with straight bangs and a ribbon tied in the top of her hair. But it said "Missing" underneath, and that made the photo kind of eerie and sad. She was an only child. Her parents ran the bakery and they had to leave for work at five o'clock in the morning. So her dad used to phone Ruth twice: once to wake her up, and then again to tell her when to leave for school. She rode her push-bike to the school in Harcourt. She had to cross the railway line and the highway. No one knew what happened to her. They never found out, not to this day. That's why it was so bad. You had to keep wondering and imagining. And the things you saw in your mind, or at least the things I saw in my mind, since I had an overactive imagination, were worse than anything, and no one could ever say, "No, it wasn't as bad as that." Once I saw a movie on telly where a man was kidnapping fat girls and keeping them in a hole and then skinning them to make coats.

Ruth Warlock wasn't big enough to be made into a skin coat. But at school there were very creepy Ruth Warlock stories going 'round. I couldn't help thinking of that pervert man holding his thing, the one Eddie and I saw. And then I started to have nightmares, because I got these two pictures stuck in my brain: Ruth Warlock, with her gap-toothed smile, and Pervert Man. They made me feel bad in my heart, and I knew then that the world wasn't safe.

That summer, we used to hang out in the gas station, where you could play Space Invaders, or in the sawmill, where you could smoke. Someone had put a mattress down in the old mill shed, so people went and pashed in there. I never did. I wasn't going to pash on some smelly mattress. Susie did. She liked those tough boys: the Nelson brothers and Froggo and Beggsie. But I didn't. Those tough guys had mean ideas. After the bushfires, Angie Hill saved this baby rabbit and kept it as a pet, and some of them shot it in the head and then gave it back to her. They thought that was funny. Once they got their driver's licenses, they spent their weekends spotlighting or paddock bashing, and they shot at the signs all the way along the road to Bendigo.

I wasn't thrilled about the scene in the sawmill, so I was really just waiting for summer to be over. I was doing my waiting under a tree in our paddock, near where Travis Houghton had his caravan. It was a mighty good tree, a claret ash, its branches crammed with leaves, spreading out and hanging low like a big old henna hairdo. If you lay underneath it and looked up, you felt better just for watching the waving leaves and the slivers of blue sky, and for letting that be the only thing in your mind, so your mind could just sway along with the weight of the branches. But my mind always got on to something. A notion could sweep it up and stir it 'round and drag it one way or another, and then I'd just float off, figuring that life would be better if I was a bird and not a girl with a bung leg and bad thoughts. I got a feeling for that tree. I took it on as a new friend. That tree didn't do me any harm at all.

The first time I got an inkling about Harry was one of those stinker summer days when I was under the tree and Eddie came out to smoke a cigarette. He squatted down with his elbows on his knees.

"You having fun?" he said.

"What?" I waved my hand in front of my nose to get rid of the smoke. I was in a purist phase.

"I said, are you having fun?" It wasn't a proper question. He wasn't even looking my way.

"What does it look like?"

He didn't answer me, so I closed my eyes and I figured he'd just leave, but he didn't.

"Eddie, are you smoking pot?" I said. "You're stoned, aren't you?"

"Look, Mannie, what're you doing here, anyway? You look like you've expired or something." He sat down properly, and I got the sense that he did have a purpose after all.

picture of me wishing I
was a tree.

OR

picture of tree not wishing.

it was me.

"Just looking up at the tree." I was lying on my back with my arms under my head. I got up onto my elbows, since I could tell we were in for a conversation. "Why, whaddya think I'm doing here?" Eddie was looking straight ahead and shaking his head as if he was disapproving.

"You think too much."

"You know that picture in the hall? Eddie?" He didn't reply. He was busy taking a deep drag on his cigarette, and he held the smoke in for as long as he could.

"Mannie, ever since your back got bad you've been lying around and thinking, and it doesn't do you any good. That's all. You get stuck inside your head. It makes you weird."

"Did you hear what I said? About the painting?" I sat up straight.

"Which, the yellow one?"

"Yeah. Why are you smoking anyway? It's bad for your lungs."

"'Cause I like it. I just like it. See, Mannie. That's exactly what I'm saying. If you didn't sit around thinking all the time, being smart about everything, then you might find you like more stuff. Problem with you is you always figure out what's wrong with things, instead of just doing them. Why don't you do something stupid? Even if it doesn't make sense, you might just enjoy it. You figure it out too much and then there's no living left to do, 'cause you've worked it all out in your head."

"Jumping off that wall was stupid."

Eddie put his hands to his forehead and then he rubbed his brow with his fingers, as if he was suddenly weary.

"Look, I know this is really going to make you mad, but I'm going to say it anyway. Sometimes you remind me of Mum. The way you float around, living inside your head, imagining things, and you get all the proportions wrong. You blow things up and you put in colors when there aren't colors, and then you can't really see what's in front of you. Did you notice it was holidays? Did you think about that? You're too busy worrying up these problems in your head. Tell you what I think, you should bloody well smoke a number. You know what I'm saying? You should make a few mistakes. Real mistakes. You know what I'm saying, Mannie?"

"Have you finished?" I said, because I never appreciated it when people tried to tell me what to do and what not to do. I pulled a bunch of old leaves up under my nose and smelled them. "I mean, is that what you came out here to say?"

"Nope, I came out to ask you if you wanted to come for a swim with me and Harry up at Wally's dam."

"You know that yellow picture I was talking about?" I persisted. Eddie puffed on his cigarette and nodded. "Well, I was thinking how it would be good to know what you were meant to do. You know how there's all those men working in that yellow field, and they're lying down, resting? I think they look like they're a part of something, and they know what their particular part is. That's why they can just go and rest like that, because they know it's their time for a spell. Do you know what I mean?"

Eddie squinted. He tapped on his cigarette and watched the ash fall.

"What would you do, Eddie? I mean, if there was no one telling you what to do?"

He shook his head. He didn't even take the time to think about it. He pushed the butt into the ground and then laid it in the palm of his hand, like a gift.

"God knows," he said as he got up. He went to walk away, but then he turned around. "You coming for a swim or not?"

"Yeah, I'm coming," I said, only because it was so damn hot, not because I needed their company.

Then again, you wouldn't ever swim alone at Wally's dam because of the leeches. Wally was a German pig farmer, and some folks said the dam had pig poo in it, but I don't think that was true. It was just the leeches. If you got one on you and there was no one to check you from behind, it would give you the creeps. That hot day I got a leech on the back of my leg and Harry burned it off with his Winnie blue. Eddie was the one who spotted it.

"Hey, you got a leech on your leg, Mannie," he said, but he wasn't jumping up to help, even though he knew how I hated leeches.

I wheeled around in a panic, and Harry just took his cigarette out of his mouth, kneeled down behind me, and took my ankle in his hand. He held the cigarette right over the leech till it dropped.

"There, it's gone," he said and he looked up at me. He didn't just let my leg drop either, he placed it back down on the ground, carefully, as if my leg was valuable. He sat down and put the cigarette back in his mouth. His hair was wet from swimming, but you could still see the curls in it.

"Mannie's got a thing about leeches," said Eddie, playing with a bucket on the end of his foot. "She's a wuss."

Harry grinned but he didn't laugh. He didn't make fun of me at all. He leaned back on his elbows and looked up at the sky or the tall gum trees with their dangling leaves. I didn't know which. It was hard to tell just what Harry had on his mind. He never said. Not like Eddie, who always told you what his opinion was, even if you didn't care to hear it.

But I knew something about Harry Jacob then. I knew that he wasn't one of those tough guys, and he'd never kill a pet rabbit. He was different.

chapter eleven

I was at the train station, waiting for the Brunswick train. I was eating a green pear, actually. I had a pear-eating method. First I ate around the top, and then I lifted it up, dangling it like a light bulb, while I tilted my head to get underneath to the fat bottom. From this position I noticed a young man watching me intently. I wouldn't have paid any attention, except that he looked so pleased with himself, as if he knew something that no one else knew. He wasn't really a man; he was a boy dressed up as a man. He was wearing a hat. A white straw hat with a black band and a dip in the middle.

It looked to me like a hat that was satisfied to have found a head that would not shy away, a head that would swagger beneath it in beaming confidence. I was busy getting lost in a haze of envy for the hat's happiness, when I noticed that the boy underneath it was looking back at me, so I smiled and explained that I was looking at his hat. I threw the pear core onto the tracks. He tipped his hat and looked up at it as if he and the hat were friends. "What's with the dress?" he said. "You going to a party? I mean it's a nice dress." I wiped my mouth on my arm.

"Actually, I am going to a party. Later." I stared out at the tracks because I was lying and I don't like to look at people when I tell a lie. He hardly seemed to notice. He stuck his hands deep in his pockets and rocked back and forth.

"Well I'm going to Queenscliff. Have you ever been there? 'Cause if you haven't you should go. You can come with me if you want to."

"No thanks. I've got stuff I have to do here."

"What stuff?"

"Just stuff.'"

"Well, there's a beach there. Maybe you should come anyway, I wouldn't care."

"Why should I?" I gave him a long look. The idea that I should do anything other than what I planned made me feel uncomfortable. He didn't say anything. He shrugged. I watched him for a moment and then I smoothed down my dress and leaned back into the wall, letting my new silver shoes peep out. I had no intention of taking up the conversation again; I didn't like the way he seemed to think he knew more about what I should do than I did.

He said, "Maybe you never been surfing, huh?"

"No, I haven't."

"You scared?"

"I'm not scared. I just don't want to go." I wasn't meant to just give up my plans and go somewhere with a random guy like him. The idea of it made me mad. He was mistaken. "Why are you asking me? Don't you have some friends you can ask?" It was as if I'd thrown something hard out at him. His head jerked back and he frowned. But he regained himself quickly and laughed.

"Don't worry. There's a whole lot of us going up for the day. I only asked you 'cause I thought you might like to hang out." He shrugged again and he said, "Have fun at your party." And then he spun around on his heel and walked up the platform a bit. I could tell he didn't like me much anymore.

I have to admit it, I felt bad, and my thoughts went over and over it. What had he seen in me that made him think I might need some friends? And why had I been so mean to him? I didn't want to be recognized and he seemed to think he had recognized me. But I was in disguise. I wasn't that old Mannie Clarkeson, I was Manon, A-type, elegant, and "on business." Probably, I reassured myself, it was just the red dress and the silver shoes, attracting attention.

The reason for my red dress was that it reminded me that I was out — not in, out. That wasn't exactly true, it was more to put me in the proper frame of mind: the outward state of mind. When I was out, I felt required by the sun, and by the trains snorting along, and by the woman with porridge legs squashed in tiger-print shoes, and even by that annoying boy, to be clean and polite. That was the outward state. Politeness didn't come naturally to me. I was really a rude person. I had rude thoughts about people. Rude and boring thoughts, actually. Not spicy, no, not that. A thought more like this:

There is a couple sitting opposite me on the train. He has short dark hair and a big chest and he is acting like a horse. She is lanky and large-nosed and wearing long pink socks for a certain effect. She wishes she could act like a horse too, but she can't. She just doesn't have it in her to act like a horse. I watched the couple a while and saw that the man didn't mind that the woman didn't have it in her to act like a horse; he must have loved her for other reasons. I wouldn't have loved her if I was that man; I just wouldn't have forgiven it. A person should be able to act like a horse if they feel like it.

I looked down at my red floating dress, which covered my legs and almost covered my silver shoes too, depending on how I placed my feet. The dress made me feel like a person in a painting: someone who wasn't actually real, someone who didn't have to wipe mud off their boots, or vacuum old carpets, or answer to anybody else. That's why I liked it. Because it exulted. In fact, the red dress effect was similar to the T-bar effect, only larger.

chapter twelve

I got off at Jewell Station. There was a map on the wall there. I pressed my thumb to it and followed the streets in my mind. Cyril Jewell House wasn't going to be hard to find. First I had to make my way to the main road. Sydney Road.

The side street from the station was crammed with buildings. It was getting hot and the air was thick and smelly. There were cars everywhere and trucks backing, causing jams. Suddenly there didn't seem to be much room. I was squeezing and squinting. The glare was bouncing off the white brick walls of a big factory. A group of three men were spread over a small stairwell, smoking cigarettes and eating falafel, so I stopped and asked if I was heading for Sydney Road.

"Like a hot chip?" One of them pushed a foam bucket of chips with sauce toward me. I shook my head. "Makes you sick, doesn't it?" he said. His hair was all greased down and he had a lazy kind of voice.

"What? The chips?" I said.

"Nuh. The government. It's fucked."

He fixed me with an uncomprehending stare, which I pretended not to notice. I figured he'd been living next to traffic too long.

Sydney Road eventually led to Sydney, if you kept heading north for another thousand Ks, so it was a big road with a lot of promise. There were shops on either side. Not special spiffy shops, like in the city, but all kinds of plain, ugly places spilling along like a crowd of jabbering orphans tossed out to the far edge of the city. The shops sold things from other parts of the world: carob paste, flat bread, artichokes, semolina cake, spinach triangles, haloumi cheese in jars, pipes with cord, rose water, and puffy white wedding dresses. Except for the wedding shops, there was no fuss about anything. Plain as plain it was, and cheap too. I felt a sudden rush of enthusiasm, to be standing in the middle of the busy footpath, buoyed up and surrounded by the grimy but half-exotic atmosphere. It was hectic and loud and gusty with smells and sounds. No one was wearing expensive shoes, I was sure.

What I liked about Melbourne was the way you couldn't ever know it. It was the hugeness of it, the gray flat streets that reached out and crisscrossed and yielded lines of houses, all proud, upright, brimming with roses and sheltered by fences. I only knew our grandparents' street and the house that stood opposite theirs. Once we'd met the boy, Paul, who lived there with his Yugoslavian mother. Paul had fat lips and hair like a helmet, and he only read *Mad* comics. I called him Paul Slop-a-lot because he had a Yugoslavian surname that sounded like that.

The last time I went to my grandparents', they'd moved to a small flat. Benjamin was dying. Dad took me and Eddie. He stood behind us as we waited at the door, one hand on each of our shoulders, as if he was about to push us forward, like little boats. We were like a package, the three of us waiting at the door. It was good to be a package since it meant that whatever was about to happen would happen to all of us together and not just me. I listened to the hiss of wet leaves scurrying into gutters, and then the murmurs of people inside.

Cully opened the door, and when she saw us she started to cry. Cully made my dad Christmas cake every year. She helped my grandparents with ironing and cooking. Sometimes she gave us old mints wrapped in tissue.

There was the smell of wet wool coats and whiskey. My shoes sank in the fat cream carpet. Aunt Marjorie stood peeping out from the kitchen door, nibbling on a cracker. Ivy tottered toward us, hands clamping around Dad's wrist, like a drowning swimmer clutching at a life raft. She didn't say much; her mouth was wobbly. Dad made excuses for why Mum wasn't with us. Ivy was wearing a long turquoise blue dress; she always wore blue, it was her color. But she'd got her makeup wrong, like a kid who can't color in properly and goes over the lines, and so she looked like a frail, disheveled queen.

"Your grandfather wants to see you. He's in the bedroom," she said, bending down to kiss us so you could smell the powder on her face. She dabbed at her eyes with a tissue. Usually Ivy took us to the kitchen, gave us biscuits or ice cream and lemonade and made a big fuss about us. Benjamin let us play with the ice dispenser on the freezer, which had a button so you could choose crushed ice or ice cubes. Eddie and I walked toward the bedroom. We'd never walked toward it like this before. It seemed to take ages. The bedroom door was half open, like a frowning mouth; it seemed hesitant, and injured, as if waiting to be properly shut or properly opened. Eddie edged in first without touching it, and I followed.

Benjamin was lying on his bed. Once, that bed had been enormous, but now, in the small room, it looked cramped, like a proud animal in a small cage. Once, it had been the center of a big room in a big house, with windows that jutted out and a line of cushions to sit on. The cushions were bleached pale by the sun, and there were dried-up insects behind the curtains. There was a grand piano in the entrance hall and hot towel rails in the bathrooms. It was a white house, solemn and tall, clean and glorious like a bride.

That white house had stood for something, something sugary and unbelievable, something that faded on the tip of your tongue like the icing dusted on Ivy's half-moon biscuits. The biscuits were kept in a tin that was hard to open. You had to take it to Benjamin in the den.

He opened the tin and let you have as many as you liked. When you kissed him, you could taste whiskey.

Now Benjamin and Ivy were on a pension and they lived in a flat in Brunswick.

Eddie announced us as we entered the bedroom.

"Benjamin, it's me and Manon."

We always called him Benjamin. He was too tall to be a grampa, never hobbling around or craggy or bent over by close-knit cardigans.

Benjamin and Ivy. Once, the two of them lay propped up by big square pillows, sitting in the four-poster bed with initialed robes and spectacles, trays of tea and toast, smelling the way grandparents do, syrupy and delicate, always happy to hoist you up there with them.

Now Benjamin lay there alone, evaporated and pale.

"Oh, it's you, my boy," he said. His head lifted a little, then dropped down. "And Manon." Skin drooped across his neck like an old curtain. He wore a gray suit, and no shoes, just clean camel-colored socks. It was almost his ninety-fourth birthday. Benjamin always did things properly, elegant as an ironed silk handkerchief, even as he died.

His hand reached for us and you could see the bones and lilac veins poking through. The hand flailed like a flapping moth, looking for someone's. Eddie pressed it between his palms.

"I'm gone, I'm gone," said Benjamin. His eyes showed only a faint look of alarm, as if even that, the fear of going, was fading. Breath wheezed in and out slowly, a whistling sound, as if it was catching and dragging over a surface. There were medical contraptions on the bedside table: white plastic things with lips and valves, and also pills. Eddie clamped down on his hand. To stop him slipping away. If only you could, hold someone there in life.

I'm gone, I'm gone. The words clawed at the stillness in the room.

"It'll be all right," said Benjamin. It was what we were supposed to say.

"Yeah," said Eddie. I didn't say anything. I don't know why. I was thinking too hard. And I didn't want to say the wrong thing. So I shut my mouth and remembered Benjamin's once-proud peppery old hands holding a hardback book up to his face. Biographies, he only read biographies. He only liked true things.

Benjamin looked at us both, his eyes flitting between us. I thought I might not ever see him again and it made me cry. But it was okay because even Eddie had tears rolling down his nose. You hardly ever saw Eddie cry.

"Did you read that book yet, Manon?" he asked. I'd forgotten about that book. A hardback biography, of course. It was about a woman, and he thought I would like her. From the photos inside it looked as if she was just a housewife called Janet. I didn't plan to be a housewife, so I'd stuck it on the bookshelf and forgotten about it.

"Not yet. But I will," I said, and I really meant it.

"Would you get me a Coke?" said Benjamin.

"Coca-Cola?" said Eddie.

"Yes." He nodded, or his chin moved inward, toward his neck.

"Okay."

As we left the room I could hear the sound of his old lame breath dragging in and out. I ran outside and sat in the gutter.

Benjamin died the next morning, in Ivy's arms. That was how he wanted it.

That night, Eddie and I climbed up on the roof of our house. Eddie went there to smoke a cigarette. I sat there to look at the sky. There was a huge motionless cloud. It felt as if something had just stopped: the forwardness of life. All the speaking, the gusts of voices, telling and asking and cutting up the silence, were just for a moment extinguished by the great sheet of darkness that rose up in the cloud. For a moment even Ruth Warlock's picture was gone from my mind. Everything had gone. There was just that dark sky curtain hanging between us and the rest — whatever the rest was. Eddie put out his cigarette.

"You thinking about Benjamin?" he said.

"No."

"Me neither."

And then the cloud passed and it became too cold to sit there. I went and dug up that book about Janet the housewife, but I didn't read it, I just smelled it.

chapter thirteen

Hope Street went downhill. A long narrow street with old weatherboard houses on either side. I hardly had to pedal, I just sat on the seat and looked at the houses going by. Nice houses, I thought, probably with nice families in them too. Cyril Jewell House sat at the end, tucked in an elbow in the road. Not far away there was a freeway, but you could only see the curved cement walls that blocked out the noise. It was a dead end, actually, and right opposite it there was a shut-up timber factory with yawning black windows and huge metal roll-up doors. Cyril Jewell House wasn't an old red house on a windy hill, as I'd imagined. It was a sprawling brick veneer with shrubby stone garden bits, tucked in a decline between the Tullamarine Freeway and Lacey's Timberwood Products. An end-of-the-line kind of place.

As I locked my bike up I could hear a wailing sound coming from one of the windows. At first it was like a hungry cat moaning for dinner, but as I listened I thought there were words in the moan.

One word repeated over and over. A person's name. It was an embarrassing, private sound. I felt I shouldn't be listening.

Inside, facing the door, was a big counter. To the right there was a very large open room. Around the edges of this room, facing inward, sat the residents. A woman in a purple quilted dressing gown sat in a wheelchair at the edge of the hall. She was neither in nor out of the room, but hovered on the edge as if she just wanted to watch from a safe distance. Leaning at the front desk was a large Maori woman talking to another woman, who held a mop over a bucket and leaned on one hip. A man walked past and popped a sweet in the mouth of the woman in purple, and the large woman interrupted her conversation to call out to him.

"That's enough, Mr. Borgello. Dorothy's had enough. No more." Mr. Borgello seemed to derive great amusement from this telling off. He giggled, hunched up his shoulders, and shuffled off down the hall.

This was almost the only activity in the whole room, despite the number of people who occupied it. They were all very old and were arranged in large padded vinyl chairs, which folded and bent and extended out like small airplanes. It looked like a very tired carnival. Quite a few of them seemed to be sleeping. Others looked out as if their eyes were just half-opened windows. I was staring at a whitish bloke in a corner who was doing a jigsaw puzzle. He lifted the pieces slowly and examined them, turning them around in his hand. He was concentrating so exactly that you could tell there wasn't a single interfering thought or doubt, and I wished I could concentrate like that. Next to him, there was a pale pink, delicately slumped woman, whose drooping head made her look like a dying hibiscus.

"Can I help you?" said the large woman. She had just caught me gawking at the old people as if they were some kind of live show of the near-dead.

"I'm here to see Ivy Clarkeson."

"Oh. You're a relative of Ivy's, aren't you?"

"She's my grandmother. But I haven't seen her for a long time. I live in the country." I felt I had to explain. She must have thought we were a terrible lot to leave Ivy alone in a nursing home and never visit. It was Mum's fault. She didn't like us to see Ivy. She said Ivy spoiled us.

"That's all right. Ivy's got photos of you and your brother on her shelf, from when you were younger. She'll be thrilled to see you. She always talks about you and Eddie. I think she's in her room. I'll take you."

We walked down a corridor. The floors were covered in gray lino and stank of piss and chlorine. I started feeling anxious. Was Ivy going to be as old and emptied-out as these people? We went past the room where the wailing was coming from. I saw a very old woman curled up on her side, lying on top of a single bed, like a pinkish shell tossed on its thin edge. She kept wailing, just as if she'd got stuck on a groove and couldn't get off. The woman called out to her as we passed. "Hello, Vera," she said, but we didn't stop.

"What's she saying?" I asked, though I could hear the words now: pain, pain, pain.

"Oh, she does it all the time. Sometimes she calls out 'I'm buggered, I'm buggered,' or some other complaint. Today it's 'pain.' Look, this is where they can get their hair done." Her large brown arm swiftly flung open a door to reveal a cell-like room with only a sink and a chair. "The hairdresser comes every month for perms or colors. And this is Ivy's room." She gave a gentle knock and then pushed open the door, saying, "Ivy, look, you've got a visitor."

Ivy sat in a big armchair next to her bed, facing the window. She wasn't reading or watching television or doing a puzzle. She was just sitting there, so still and quiet and gentle that it made you feel you ought to whisper and kneel, as if she was a holy person having a spiritual moment. An apricot and blue floral dress hung over her small, bony body, and as we entered, her thin arms moved slightly, like startled branches in a sudden gust of wind. Then she turned toward us in an awkward flurry, as if we'd woken her up. Her eyes squeezed together, trying to focus.

"What?" she said crossly, her bony hands clutching at the sides of the chair. The woman pushed me forward and whispered loudly, "It's Manon." Then she closed the door and left us.

"Manon?" said Ivy, and her voice climbed up and seemed to dissolve.

"Hi, Ivy." I bent down and took her hand. It was covered in sun spots.

"Manon?" she said again, and she gripped my hand tightly. Her other hand rose, trembling, to her mouth. She seemed pale and worried as she scanned my face. Then she turned away and looked at the window, her hand tapping at her lips.

"I thought I was dreaming," she said, and when she turned back to look at me there were tears in her pale old eyes. It did a strange thing to me, seeing Ivy then. It grabbed at my heart and made tears come to my eyes. I hadn't cried for a very long time and I felt ashamed of myself. I went red in the face and wiped my eyes and then I gazed wildly around the room, since I felt I had to do something rather than just stand there with tears in my eyes. Ivy reached for me and then I was in her arms, next to a cheek, soft and loose like an old hankie. Ivy smelled like lavender and soap, her eyes shone, and she patted the bed, indicating for me to sit down.

"Look!" she cried, pointing proudly to the bookcase. It was mainly empty except for three photo frames standing side by side and a small silver urn. There was the photo I recognized of me and Eddie, taken on Christmas Day. My arm was in a plaster cast. I'd broken it trying to fly off a rope at school. I did fly, just for a moment, outspread in the air like a swallow, like a balsa-wood-eagle show-off. Then I landed. A belly whacker. My arms cracked on the ground. I only broke one though, and I didn't cry because the whole playground was watching.

Hanging from my other hand there was that doll, Velvet. When you pressed her belly button the hair shortened, disappearing into a hole at the top of her head. You could pull the hair long again whenever you wanted, but I cut the hair with Mum's nail clippers to see if it would still grow. It didn't, and Velvet looked like a punk. When Mum saw, she said I didn't deserve to have nice things since I ruined them, but I never meant to ruin Velvet.

In the photo, Eddie was wearing red shorts and thrusting his chin forward, looking very pleased with himself, for no reason; no doll, he was just pleased. Typical of Eddie, I thought, and I sighed.

Next to that photo was Ivy's wedding photo, in black and white. Benjamin stood tall and proud, one hand holding a pair of white gloves, the other wrapped around his new wife, in an owning kind of way. Ivy held a bunch of lilies. She smiled calmly. A veil foamed around her feet. She wore an ivory satin dress with fifteen buttons on the sleeve. She'd made it herself.

I picked up the third photo. It was of my parents in a restaurant. Mum was looking at Dad; he was looking at the camera. She had a low-cut dress on and her hair was swept up. She was looking at Dad in a way I'd never seen before, as if she thought he was lovely.

"That's your parents," said Ivy, leaning forward. "That was their engagement. Before you were even born. We were at Florentino's, in the city. Did you ever go to Florentino's?"

I shook my head and replaced the photo. Ivy leaned back in her chair and gazed up at me. "Would you look at you, Manon. Can you believe it? You're so grown-up. Look at your dress. My, you look lovely, really lovely. How long since I saw you? How long?" Her hand was pressing into her chest.

"Not since Eddie —"

"Oh!" she cried. There was a sad look in her eyes and she nodded slowly. "It's a shame, darling. That's all. It's a great shame. Your mother —" Her voice evaporated into the air, while her hand clutched at her throat. Ivy was suddenly quiet.

"Ivy?"

Ivy stirred and touched my cheek.

"Manon. One day you must go there. To Florentino's. You tell Georgio who you are. Say you're Ivy and Benjamin Clarkeson's only granddaughter. He's the headwaiter. He'll remember me and Ben. We went there every anniversary. Third of May. Every one. Can you believe it?" She patted me on the knee and grinned. "Tell me, my darling, tell me, have you got a boyfriend?"

"No," I said. I wanted to say yes. I really wanted to tell Ivy about last autumn. But it was a long story and I wasn't sure a grand-mother would understand.

"No?" She laughed and patted my knee again. "You will have," she said. I steered the subject away.

"Ivy, is it all right here? I mean, do you like it?"

"Here?" cried Ivy. "Oh, my dear, no one likes it here. No one wants to be here. Oh, the nurses are very good, but no one wants to be here. My God, have you seen the dayroom? Have you seen them all sleeping there?"

"But you're not like them, Ivy."

"No, not yet. There's a couple of us here still got our wits. Me and Patricia and Bert Gammon. And Selma Blake too. Selma's all right, only she talks too much. Gives you an ache in the ear after a while." Ivy rearranged herself in the chair and nodded toward the door. "Have you seen the courtyard? They had to build the wall higher because some of them keep trying to go back home." She gave a little snort and then shrugged, her thin old elbows squawking out to the side.

"You should have been living with us, Ivy." At this Ivy's eyes glazed over, her gaze drew back within, and she stared straight ahead into space and drifted off. I watched her. Her mouth widened into a thin pale line. Ivy was an old lady now. Her face had no more padding in it. I couldn't help but see that she was near the end of her life, and it gave me a great pain in my heart. Even though I never saw her, I depended on Ivy being there. I loved Ivy in a very true way. Ivy was what gave me a family feeling, a proper family feeling, where someone hugged you and asked questions and told you that you were a beautiful girl, not hopeless. The thought of Ivy not being there was making me grip my leg so tight it hurt. When Ivy returned, her face lit up, as if she'd just seen me for the first time again.

"Hey, Ivy, let me give your feet a rub. Are they sore?"

After Benjamin died in his big blue bed, Ivy became thin and frail like a swan, and her bones seemed to give in. She was often falling over and breaking her knee or her foot. When she was in the hospital, I massaged her feet because they were infected and nothing was making them better, not the drugs or creams. She claimed only rubbing them really helped. I worried about Ivy's feet; I worried that she was losing her footing, that after all those years of being Benjamin's wife, her feet were abandoning her now. I imagined her dissolving slowly, starting at her feet. So I rubbed those feet, to coax them back, to show them the ground.

After Benjamin died in his big blue bed, the flat was sold and Ivy had to move into Cyril Jewell House. I helped her to sort out her clothes — which ones to take, which ones to give to the Salvation Army. She had four cupboards full of clothes, and each piece of clothing was a decision. To leave it behind was also to leave something of herself. She'd been the wife of a successful man, that was her role, an enviable role, which she performed with pride. There were hats. A hat for every outfit, worn once and packed away in a round box, wrapped in shadows and time. Ivy and I had opened each one as if it was a gift, a new strange flower that contained within its veils, ribbons, edges, and floppy brims, the faded music of another time: a carnival, glasses of champagne, a crowd of people being polite, being impolite. So we stood there in the hats, pulling out dresses and shirts (most of them still wearing the yellow smudges of spilled wine or chicken casserole), pulling out lavender dressing gowns, Chinese silk pajamas, beaded handbags. And then there was the wooden chest of drawers, the one she was leaving till last.

Once, as a child, I'd found a set of false teeth in the top drawer. I ran downstairs, holding the teeth in the palm of my hand like an inexplicable insect I had found in the garden. I shouted, "Look, teeth, teeth, I found teeth!"

Ivy had been embarrassed. She had quietly taken them and put them away and not explained the teeth at all. She had simply said that I should not look in those drawers because they were private. Private. I whispered the word. It excited me.

She didn't go to the top drawer. She kneeled down and opened the bottom drawer and pulled out, one by one, a suite of sumptuous nightgowns and black lace slips. She held them up to her, long satin flowing things, and thrust a pale pink one in my direction, saying she was too old for pink. She kept the rest. I never wore the pink satin nightie. It was more something Mum would have worn.

"Ooh, that's lovely, thank you," she said as I kneaded her old feet. "Tell me, how's your dad? Are you here all on your own?"

"Dad's fine. I came on my own."

"Oh, and where will you stay?"

"With a friend called Helena. A theater director!"

"A theater director," repeated Ivy vaguely and I could tell her mind had gone soft again. Perhaps the effort of talking tired her out. I sat quietly and waited for Ivy to speak. I was looking at the window with the slat blinds. There was sun coming through in thin planks. Leaves scratched by outside on the street. Ivy sighed and said how it was sad. I didn't know what it was she was referring to exactly — maybe it was the dead leaves being tossed in the gutter. I always felt sad about that myself. In fact, I bet everyone feels that good-bye feeling in autumn, especially. Autumn is the sad season, but once there's a true sadness within you, autumn will sing it soft and slow in your heart. It's because of the turning. In that last blaze of red, in the biting air and the slow drift and fall of leaves, you see the slight farewell that life is always repeating. You know you can't hold it still. You watch it go.

That last autumn I started going to the orchards after school, instead of going home. It wasn't any good at home when Eddie wasn't there. With no one to help negotiate Mum's moods, I got the full blast of them. So I just dumped my schoolbag, grabbed some biscuits, called Mou, and we went. Not only that, I didn't hang out with Lucy at the sawmill or the gas station anymore. I just didn't feel like it.

I'd always naturally liked autumn best of all the seasons. In fact, if I'd been a season instead of a girl, that's what I would have been. I wouldn't have chosen to be autumn, I'd be summer if I could, but that's not how I was. Lucy Brixton was summer. So was Eddie. But I was always autumn. I liked the gold, shaking leaves and the long slow movement of the skies and the bruised look of summer sinking away. Summers were fierce and bright, blasting down over the fields, turning the grass into a crackly straw and drying up the creek. It was too hot to walk up the dirt road in summer, but by the time apple season came, it was too cool for swimming and just right for walking. It was glowing and fresh outside, and you could walk anywhere and not have to worry about flies or sunburn or snakes.

The apple trees stood in long lines. It was best up the back, near the surrounding bush, where the trees were older and larger, with bigger canopies. There were pear trees there too, and you couldn't see any roads, just the bush and the cold storage shed and the big stack of wooden crates that sat on top of the hill like a badly built castle. The young trees at the front lined the roads and had their middles cut out of them and their branches pruned in funny U shapes. They looked as if they were reaching their arms up, waiting for the heavens to unleash something upon them: a shower of gold or just plain forgiveness. Not that apple trees need forgiveness.

I walked down the rows looking for Eddie and Harry. Usually I could find them because of Harry's habit of whistling. He had a very good, tuneful whistle, which floated through the trees and skipped around and caught the edge of your mind, so you opened your ears and listened. And it lifted your spirits to hear a little tune like that, because it was jaunty and breezy and gave you a hopeful feeling, the feeling you get just before a holiday.

When I found them I plonked myself down on the grass and leaned back on my arms and stayed there a while. Mou gave up on the walk for a while too, and he rolled on his back or gnawed on an apple. The last shafts of sun fell between the trees. No one said much. I tugged at the grass and watched.

It didn't seem very long ago that I would have gone nuts just sitting and watching something and not being part of the action. And I wasn't sure what made me happy to just sit there and watch; it was a new, different kind of game I'd just happened upon, and it involved my head much more than my arms and legs (which suited me better now that my leg was bung). What I did with my head was I tried to clean it out, as if it was a cupboard full of stuff and I wanted it all emptied so it was ready for new things to go in. If I wiped out everything I knew, then I could look through my eyes as if I'd never seen anything before. That was when the trees started to look sad to me.

"Hey, Harry, how'd you like to be one of these poor trees, not allowed to grow its branches in its own particular shape, but being forced to look like every other tree and stand in a row and hold apples for people to eat?"

"Mannie, I'd be pretty pissed," said Harry, tossing an apple high in the air and catching it, "if I was one of these trees." And then he kept whistling. I watched Eddie for a while with my cleaned-out head, and then I watched Harry, and then I switched my eyes quickly from one to the other, just to see if they came out different in my mind.

Eddie was longer and looser than Harry. That was the first thing. He had thin arms and a long neck and tanned skin, and people said he was handsome. Eddie and I both had dark hair and eyes like our mother. His upper lip was sweating and he was squinting upward. Eddie just seemed to hang from himself as if he was only a coat he was wearing. He did everything in this easy way, hands relaxed. I knew he wasn't thinking anything much, just fixing his mind on getting apples.

Harry had taken off his shirt. Harry was more intentional than Eddie, if you know what I mean. They both had pickers' canvas bags on their fronts. Eddie was up one of those yellow steel ladders and Harry was on the ground. He had freckles on his shoulders, sprinkled all over. His body wasn't loose, like Eddie's — it was knowing and slow and direct, as if it was ready, sprung or loaded. But I couldn't tell what loaded it. Maybe it was just the way his eyes sloped down at the corners, which made him appear always slightly amused, as though there was a silent slight laughter inside him. Anyway, I liked the look in Harry's eyes when he looked straight at you. It made me smile, even though I didn't mean to.

But what I liked best was watching Harry with the apples. His arms were thicker than Eddie's, and he could catch an apple in one hand without it even making a thud. Eddie could do it too. Maybe all boys can do it, I don't know, but I especially liked watching Harry because he was different, as I said. It was as if his hand saw the apple falling and reached and fell with it; even as it wrapped around the apple the hand kept falling as if it had become the falling apple, and to the apple it must have seemed like a soft ride. That was how he could catch them, loosely and softly but also exactly. And he and Eddie got the picking and dropping and catching going in such a way that it was like watching someone getting pushed on a swing, when you can see just how the swinging feels and you get lulled by it, so that I almost stopped thinking altogether. It made me quiet.

"How's school, Mannie?" said Harry, but he didn't stop to ask. He kept working and I hardly wanted to speak myself since the thinking part of me had sunk down and almost disappeared.

"All right."

Harry lifted his arms behind his head and stretched, and I could see the hair under his arms. It was fine and long and sticking to his underarms because of the sweat. Half of it pointed up and half pointed down. What I thought was that Harry Jacob was strong and he would be able to carry someone if, for some reason, someone couldn't walk. It was funny; Harry wasn't handsome but he was something. I was trying to find a word for it, for what Harry was, and as I was searching my mind Harry looked at me, for no apparent reason. He was almost smiling but I couldn't be sure. What I did know was that he was seeing right into my thoughts. I felt myself blushing and looking back at him as if I could see into his thoughts too, and if Harry saw the blush he didn't say, and I didn't either, but both of us must have seen that something had happened. The way we knew each other had just slipped and turned the way a season begins to turn and slip into another.

chapter fourteen

I should have known something was brewing with Mum. She was suddenly happy that autumn. She was like a girl. We even went shopping for a winter coat, all the way to Myer at Bendigo. We got a blue coat with wooden buttons that slipped into cord loops and reminded me of the thing you wind a kite string on. She let me choose it myself. I could tell she didn't much like the duffle coat, but at least she didn't say it was ugly. She went off and bought stockings. I saw Susie Newbound in Bendigo. She was having a smoke. She didn't say anything about my new coat. She wasn't very fashionable herself. Susie was working behind the bar at the Albion Hotel. She didn't look hugely pregnant, just a bit bigger than usual. I said I didn't think you were meant to smoke when you were pregnant, but Susie said she couldn't give it up now. She told me about a party on Saturday night in Castlemaine, but I didn't want to go anyway. Not that I had other plans.

I was wearing in the new duffle coat in the car on the way home. It had a hood, but I didn't wear the hood. We were going along the

Midland Highway and a train was suddenly alongside us on the tracks, making such a loud noise we couldn't even hear the radio. Mum looked at me and she was grinning.

"Shall we beat it?"

"Okay," I said, and with that she tossed her head back and laughed, like a horse about to bolt. She leaned forward and made the car go so fast that I held on to the seat. Her hair was blowing about and she kept taking her hand off the wheel to tuck her hair back, but it didn't stay. She was excited, racing, racing the train. I hardly ever saw her like that, but when I did it was good. Her eyes were laughing and the train was roaring and the steering wheel was shaking and I was sticking my head out the window, my face wide in the mad pressing *whoosh* of air, and I was laughing too. And when it finished, when she had to brake at our road, she hooted the horn at the train and she looked at me, a calm and insistent triumph in her eyes.

"We won," she said. I nodded, because I did feel for a minute that we'd won. Not the race, but something else. We'd won over the distance that was jammed between us. We'd tripped up and landed side by side. For a minute we were together in life; for a reckless wild minute we laughed the same laugh, and I wished it could always be like that.

I didn't know what she was planning.

·　·　·　·　·

I was walking up the road on my way home. Once daylight saving was over, if you stayed back at school or if you hung out anywhere, you could feel the air, rustling and furtive, turning dark and cold. I liked this feeling: the earth preparing for change, the whispering flutter of the trees, the soft gold wedge of light beckoning from windows, saying come, come and be warmed. There was a smell, a damp smell of dirt and life, of tramped-on leaves, of steam coming off soups, of animals and dew, of plans life was making, of restless darknesses ribboning out and infusing the air with promise. Every year it smelled the same, and it was a nose memory; you remembered something, just vaguely, not a specific event, more a time, a sense of a time that leaves and returns, leaves and returns. Noses have softer, larger, fuzzier ways of remembering. They're like animals.

Harry Jacob and his dog, Blue, were walking along the road, coming toward me. Just him and Blue. I'd never seen Harry on his own. It was always with Eddie that I saw Harry. I wasn't even sure I wanted to see Harry on my own, but I'd definitely been imagining what would happen if we did. The minute I knew it was him I got a bad attack of the funnies. (The funnies was what me and Lucy called the icky feeling you got around boys, especially if they put their arm around you or tried to hold your hand. It made you shiver.) That wasn't at all how I imagined it. I tried to walk nicely, not to limp.

"Hi," said Harry.

"Hi," I said back. "Where're you going?"

He leaned his head to the side and squinted into the sun, which was sinking over the railway bridge behind me. He had his hands in his pockets and he swayed a little.

"To the tunnel. Wanna come?"

"Why you going to the tunnel?"

"You'll see," he said and he didn't seem too concerned whether I came or not. So I tagged along. We walked toward the bridge, the two of us, and it felt funny to be walking along with Harry, as if it was he and I who were friends and not he and Eddie.

"Where's Eddie?" I said.

"Footy," said Harry.

Everything seemed to be shining with trueness. The sky, the ground, the distance. Puddles of sinking sun lay in the paddocks. The trees cast long, proud shadows and the tall grasses glittered in appreciation, as if basking in the glory of it all. A flock of parrots flew over us and I could hear the *whoosh* of their wings. The air was full of sighing, as if it was sinking down and settling, like a sheet flung over the earth in rest.

Harry led us up Blackjack Road and then along the path that followed the train tracks. We turned down and went under the bridge, and he leaned up against the wall. It was a narrow tunnel, with curved brick walls on either side and a thin trail of wet along the bottom. Inside it was cool and echoey.

"Is this all you wanted to show me, Harry? 'Cause I've already been here plenty of times," I said as I leaned against the opposite wall. Harry glanced down at his watch.

"It isn't a thing to see, Mannie. It's a thing to feel. Wait, will you. Another few minutes."

I didn't care what it was, anyway. I wasn't getting the funnies anymore. I was getting something else.

"Eddie's going 'round with Alison Porrit," I said.

"I know."

"He's dead keen." I don't know why I said that. Eddie wasn't dead keen on anybody. He just liked Alison because she was pretty.

Harry didn't answer me. He was looking up at the roof and running his finger along where the drips were coming down.

"Did he tell you?"

"Tell me what?" Harry squatted down on his heels; his hair fell over one eye and he blew it off.

"Did he tell you 'bout Alison?"

"Yeah. He told me." Harry grinned and I didn't know what he was grinning at but it must have been something.

"What do you know, Harry?" I said, sliding down the wall so I was looking at him eye to eye.

He raised his eyebrows as if he was going to tell me, but then he was distracted. "Hey! You hear that?" He jerked his head behind him. It was a train's whistle. "It's the goods train." Harry stood up, so I did too. The sound was drumming through the tracks all the way.

It came louder and louder and the mounting of the roar got me excited; it boiled up your blood with the sense of something frightening and violent and mad charging toward us. But underneath it there was not a sound, there was nothing that even whimpered or budged in our tunnel and it seemed Harry and me were tightly sealed inside something, like two secret letters lying next to each other in an envelope. Harry looked up at the roof as the train went over. He laughed, but I couldn't hear the laugh, I could only hear the train going over us. I laughed too. It was so loud it was funny. And then, just as quick as it came, the noise started to sink away. We stood still and listened, the way you watch someone walk away. We watched with our ears.

"Worth it?" said Harry, when the noise had completely gone.

"Yeah." We looked outside the tunnel, back over the paddocks and trees, which were still and quiet as ever. The cows had their heads bent down to the grass, and were just chewing away like they always were. The trees were looking all important, black and tall, composed and unworried by the layering tumble of days upon them. And just looking at them like that did a strange thing to me. First, there was this unfamiliar quietness, as if I'd never before really heard a quietness, or listened to it. For an instant, a great endless space opened up in my mind, but not only my mind, in the whole of me, and into that lovely startling stillness poured the truth of those trees, and that sky and the cows and the whole thing, the whole mysterious sense of it. I couldn't hold it there, though, since the instant I recognized it, my mind jumped up and down with excitement and trampled all over it. I stared in a wild way, wondering what it was, what was there in the world that lay at your feet so quiet and beautiful that it couldn't be held by any part of you. I was lit up, and I wanted to tell, but it wasn't tellable. It couldn't fit into words. I was feeling I could have been a tree myself, and though it was almost the finest feeling I'd ever had, I made myself look down at my shoes so that I'd stop brimming with treeness, in case I looked funny and Harry might think I was a nutcase, not a tree.

What I did know was that I'd had a moment of pure happiness. The day had gone, the noise and goings-on subsided, and the last throw of light was like a curtain coming down on the end of the show. I felt as though I should clap and cry "encore," but I restrained myself and wondered instead what had caused that happiness. I couldn't be sure if Harry had caused it or not, or if the noise of the train had caused it, or if I'd just caused it myself. So I didn't let on about it. I didn't even look straight at Harry. He walked me all the way back to my house and I raced inside to make sure he didn't feel obliged to say good-bye in a meaningful way.

When I got inside, I could hear music coming from the living room. I could hear my mother laughing. The rest of the house was dark. I went in but she didn't hear me. She was there with Travis

Houghton. They were standing opposite each other and he had his arm on her waist. She was throwing her head back, laughing. When she laughed she always threw her head back, her hair spreading down like molasses. She was wearing lipstick and hoop earrings and a flared red skirt. The record was still going around. Travis was in his work clothes and his hands were dirty. He saw me. He dropped his hand from my mother's waist and wiped his mouth.

"Look, it's Manon," he said, taking my mother by her shoulders and turning her toward me. She smiled.

"Hello, darling. Look, I'm trying to teach Travis to dance but he's hopeless." Then she smiled up at Travis. She never called me darling. I think it was a mistake.

"You're really hopeless, you know?" she said to him, and by the way she giggled you could tell that she didn't mean it badly, not like how she meant it when she said it to me. He laughed and flopped down on our couch, as if he was in his own living room, as if he was staying around. His dirty hands rested over the back of our new couch.

"Isn't Eddie home yet?" I said to Mum.

"Eddie? No, he's at footy training."

"Where's Dad?"

She frowned and stamped her foot. She was wearing high heel shoes. She said I knew very well where my father was. He was at work still. She prodded a pile of magazines and acted as if she were arranging them more neatly, as if she were being a housewife. Then she turned and smiled again at Travis.

"You're home late, Manon," he said, and I didn't like the way his eyebrows moved.

"Mmm," I said, and then I went and turned on all the other lights in the house. What I really wanted was to go and think about Harry, but I was irritated by Travis and I wouldn't relax until he left our house.

chapter fifteen

Ivy took my hand and held it between hers. There was great sadness on her face. I knew what she was thinking and I didn't want to talk about that. I had other things I wanted to talk about.

"Ivy?" I said quickly. "What went wrong with Mum?"

"Why did she run off, you mean?"

"No. I mean is she schizo? Is she mad?" After my mum ran off with Travis Houghton, she was never herself again. She rang up from Melbourne where she was living with Travis. Eddie didn't want to speak to her. It put him in a bad mood.

"Mad? No. Not mad. She's unwell. She's unbalanced. Manon, I should tell you, your mother never liked me very much. We never got on very well, she and I. I don't know whose fault that was; I'm not blaming her for that. There's a lot of things I do blame her for, mind you, but not that." She paused as if to give time to that revelation, though I'd known it anyway.

"Your father's a very good man," she said. "He always was, but he's not fancy, he's not an ambitious man. By God, he fell for your mother, though. You know, marrying her was the most ambitious thing he ever did."

"Why? Why was that ambitious?"

Ivy looked up at the ceiling and considered a way to explain it. She scratched her head.

"Well, it was like a dog marrying a cat. Anyone could see how different they were. Not that that's always a bad thing. But in this case it was. See, your dad's a gentle, loving man. Your mum, she was complicated."

"How did they meet?" Of course I'd heard the story before, from them, but I wanted to hear it again, from another angle.

"He was studying Vet Science at the time he met her. He had a friend, this fellow, Sam Wheeler. Sam was in promotions. He drove a big car and he had this big laugh, you could hear him a mile off. I don't know what he saw in your dad. Ned was always a quiet one, but he and Sam were good mates. Anyway, it was Sam's fault that Ned met your mother. Sam took him to a party, it was something to do with that theater company — the French one. Your mother was there. It was only a couple of weeks later they were engaged."

Ivy nodded to the photo on the bookshelf. "Ned was as happy as I'd ever seen him. She was too, at first."

I looked at that photo. I remembered my dad, the way he used to toss a piece of fruit in the air and catch it with a snap, as if he were pleased with the way things were about him — the blue air, the market vegetables in a big basket on the table, eggs cooking, Saturday.

And Mum, she was happy when there were other people there. She would giggle and serve milk in the pale green jug and butter placed in a neat slab on a little glass dish. And she put fresh flowers everywhere, even in the bathroom.

"I don't know what it was, why I didn't have a good feeling for it," Ivy said in a musing way. Then, as if she'd caught something out of the thin air and snapped it into shape, she clapped her brittle old hands together and cocked her head. "You know what I think, to tell you the truth, I think she wanted a chance to leave something behind her in France and start again here. We had money then, Benjamin was doing well and she saw that Ned, well . . . Love, look, I'm not saying she was a gold digger, she wasn't that; it was something else she wanted from Ned. Perhaps it was just that he loved her so and she was taken with his devotion. That kind of love can seem so safe."

I'd never thought of Dad as being a good man, because he didn't shine; he didn't do anything that you'd notice. Nothing you could boast about at school. Not like being an actress. That was something.

"But it didn't suit your mother's nature," said Ivy, nodding her head as if agreeing with herself. "Your mother was a real drama queen. She loved to create drama around her. She also liked the finer things in life. She had ambitions; she wanted some kind of glory. Oh, you should have seen the clothes she used to buy. And he never even complained. She'd walk around town dressed to the nines. It wasn't appropriate, not in a country town. She drew attention, people talked about her. . . . Manon, there's something you should know."

Ivy leaned forward and I could see the skin sagging on her neck. What she said after that made me feel very bad, and I remember I was looking at the floor as she said it and I was thinking it was the ugliest floor I'd ever seen and why should old dying people have to put up with ugly floors. Shouldn't you have a lovely thing to look at when you've lived a whole lifetime and put up with all the lumps that life heaps on top of you and still got to the end of it? It made me angry, that floor.

"So she is schizo, isn't she?" I said, kicking the foot of Ivy's chair.

"Oh no. You mustn't worry about it now. Of course, she'd never planned to live in the country. When she married Ned she thought they'd be living here in Melbourne, but then Ned accepted a position in Castlemaine. He'd always imagined a quiet life and he assumed she would like it too. But she hated it. She always used to say she was living the wrong life. Do you remember? Ned should have brought her back to Melbourne, but he didn't. Perhaps he knew by then that she'd never be happy, wherever she was."

"Ivy, do you think she'll ever come back?" I fixed my eyes on the ugly floor and my voice came out in crumbs.

"Oh, my dear, is this upsetting you? You mustn't let it. She may well come back. Don't think of her as bad. She was a very charming woman, when she wanted to be. She was right in a way. She was just living the wrong life. I think when people get stuck in situations that go against their soul, they can't be happy. That's all."

I turned and stared out the window. I couldn't see anything out there, only slits of light coming through the venetian blinds. I closed my eyes for a second and let the light slide across my face, like it did under the apple trees.

There's a photo of my mother, an old black-and-white photo that was stuck in the front of the photo album, and every time anyone looked in the album, that was the biggest, most memorable photo. It was a proper one, taken by a photographer in France, where she used to live. In it, she is sitting on a surfboat, right at the peak: white bikini, ankles crossed, toes dainty and balancing her on the boat's edge, one hand carelessly thrown up to hold her sunhat on. There's a line of men with their hands on the boat, all smiling like idiots, their eyes in a join-the-dots line straight toward her, looking like they're about to push the boat out over the waves with just my mother sitting on the bow like a figurehead. My mother is laughing, of course. All those men. She always laughed around men. The photo was set up, you could tell. But she really was like that. She liked a lot of attention.

I turned back to Ivy. I told her that there was no way in the world I was getting stuck in any situation that went against my soul, and Ivy said she knew it was so, and I heaved a big sigh. Ivy leaned her head back in her chair and closed her eyes and opened her mouth just a little so the breaths could come out. And in the quietness that fell between us, I knew that something had been done, not done and finished, but done and started, like when you cast on the first line of knitting and see how big the jumper will be. I couldn't get a picture of what kind of thing was being knitted, but I felt sure that until it was knitted there'd be a large part of me that would stay cold.

chapter sixteen

After the tunnel, I stopped going to the orchards because I didn't want Harry to think I was going there to see him. I didn't trust myself to be normal and natural since I'd started having feelings about Harry Jacob. Even Eddie might notice and he'd stir me to death if he knew. I couldn't ever control my feelings, couldn't tell how they'd make me behave. It was as if the feelings I had for Harry were once just plain-colored feelings, but now they'd darkened and reddened and brightened too, and whatever I did or said would have to come out in this bright red way. I tested it out on Lucy at school.

"Hey, what d'you think of Harry Jacob?" I blurted this out in a very red manner; there was no easy way in.

"Harry Jacob?" Lucy didn't seem to notice anything. She can be really dense about some things.

"You know, Eddie's friend."

"The one with curly hair?"

"Yeah, him."

She nodded and took her time to think about it. "I've never

spoken to him. He's shy, isn't he?" she declared. "Why? Do you fancy him?"

"No. It's just, he's different, you know, he isn't a tough guy. He's nice."

She nodded. "What does he do, though? Isn't he just picking apples?"

"Yeah."

"Hey, is Eddie still going 'round with Alison?"

"I s'pose so. You never know with Eddie."

"Are you coming to see *Star Wars* on Friday? Is Eddie coming?"

"Probably. Yeah."

Star Wars was a big event in Castlemaine, and that was when I saw Harry again. It ended up almost like a date, in a back-door kind of a way. Harry was driving his brother's truck. He was taking Eddie. Eddie said I could squeeze in the front with them. But then Alison Porrit wanted to come too. So Eddie decided he'd get the bus with Alison, and that left me to go with Harry.

"Do you mind, Mannie?" said Eddie. "Harry said he'd still pick you up and take you."

"I don't mind," I said with a sigh, as if I was just being obliging. "I'll go with Harry."

So there it was. Almost a proper date. I let myself believe it was, and I made a special effort to look nice. I washed my hair and even dried it with a hair dryer. I put on some of Mum's lipstick and kissed a tissue and tossed it in the bathroom bin. There were always bits of kissed Kleenex, which Mum left around in the bathroom. I didn't know the reason for this practice, but I did it anyway since Mum knew a lot more than I did about the craft of dressing up. If there was one thing my mum gave a lot of attention to, it was making herself look nice. She didn't sweep the floor much, but she always looked nice.

When Harry arrived I was still in the bathroom. So I had to make an entrance into the kitchen, where Mum and Harry stood warming their backs at the stove. I'm not one for entrances.

"Oh, Manon, look what you're wearing," cried Mum, rolling her eyes in despair. "You look like an orphan. Isn't that some underwear?" I frowned and looked at Harry, who was wearing a jacket, and then back at my mother. I steadied my voice.

"No, it's a jumper," I said. I knew it was a jumper. It was a thin cream-colored jumper with little holes in it.

"Manon, it's an undershirt. Where did you get it? At the underwear shop or at the thrift store?" My mother giggled as if it was a joke meant to amuse Harry. But Harry looked at the floor. I put the back of my hand to my mouth and tried to smudge off the lipstick. I suddenly felt stupid for trying to look nice. I wanted to hide the evidence of it.

"Shall we go, Harry?" I said. My cheeks were red and hot and awful, and I wanted to get away from the kitchen.

"Harry will be embarrassed to take you out," said my mother, flicking her hair. She turned toward Harry and laughed. "Lucky she's not wearing the tea cozy, Harry." Even though she didn't like Harry, she could still act like a girl with him because he was almost a man.

"I reckon Mannie looks nice whatever she wears," said Harry. He was so soft and unprotected and true that it made me want to take his hand and hold it. But I would never do that, especially not with my mother watching. I didn't feel like saying another word. I didn't want to put out another thing because I knew she'd stomp it to the ground, as if it were a new tree sucker trying to grow where it wasn't allowed. I looked at Harry half urgently.

"Let's go," I said, and after the front door was shut and we stepped off the front porch, Harry put his hand on my back for a moment as we walked to the car. I didn't look at him and he didn't look either.

Around us the birds wheeled and screeched in the fading light. The thin trees leaned and shivered over the creek and the sky glowed a dark lilac color. Just before we made it to the car we were walking close enough for me to smell the dark warm smell at his neck, and I wondered then if I might even marry Harry Jacob and never have to worry about trying to look nice again.

chapter seventeen

He didn't ring me up after that date at the movies. He just came and got me. He whistled at my window. I heard him. I knew it was him. Straightaway I knew. I felt all whizzed up. I opened the window and leaned out. He was standing by that old messy melaleuca and it was getting dark.

"Harry?" I whispered.

"Yep." He didn't move away from the tree. He was whittling something with a pocket knife.

"What are you doing?"

"Waiting."

"What for?" There was a pause and then he stepped out and handed me the thing he was whittling. It was a funny looking bird, carved out of wood, the wings tucked into the body, little holes for eyes. I had it on the palm of my hand. I didn't know what to think. I wasn't sure I liked it.

"You made a bird?" I said.

He nodded. "Wanna go for a drive, Mannie?" His hands were in his pockets and he was looking straight at me.

"Where to?" I put the bird on the windowsill since I wasn't sure if he was giving it to me or not.

"I dunno. Maybe the Springs."

"Okay. Wait. I'll come out the back door."

As if I cared where we'd go. But you have to ask. You can't sound too unconditional. So I just went. I had this urge to go and tell Eddie what I was doing, but I didn't. I just went.

Vaughan Springs is really a river fed by springs. There's old pumps with taps where you used to be able to get the spring water, but now you can't. So it's not just any old river. It's a special place, where people in the gold rush used to picnic. Once there was a small train for kids, but now there's just the tracks. There's a slide, though, and a path alongside the river.

We were walking by the river. I knew there was no particular reason to be walking; we weren't going anywhere, we were just walking. The walking was like an excuse. If we weren't walking then there'd be nothing except me and him. Just me and him and no action or reason or filling. So we were just going along beside each other so that the space between us could draw close, surreptitiously, if you know what I mean. On the other side of the river was a steep bank covered in toothy dark trees that seemed to rise toward a gaping sky. On our side there was a wide plain and rows of old elm trees planted long ago. The trees swayed a little and there was a whispering sound coming from the leaves and a rushing sound from the river. I was cold. Harry gave me his coat. I said he didn't have to but he gave it to me anyway. I could smell him in the coat.

Walking alone with Harry Jacob was the best thing in the world, and I couldn't imagine how one single fish in the sea could at that moment be as happy as me. Nothing would ever matter again. Even if I never ever got to do something special, like be in a theater company, I wouldn't care.

Harry was explaining how they were replanting the original river red gums along the banks. You could see them, protected by old milk cartons. I looked over but I wasn't really noticing what he was saying since I was busy thinking how strange it was that nothing else mattered, nothing except walking along by the dark river with him. Even now I can still picture the trees reaching up into the night and spreading their fragrance in soft invisible clouds. As if love had enlarged the shape of things, made the whispering of the leaves more insistent, amplified the quiet emptiness of the path, unleashed the darkness and offered it to us alone.

"It's strange," I said, but I didn't really mean to say it.

"What's strange?" said Harry and he bent down and picked up a leaf and folded it in half.

I didn't answer. I hadn't meant to test the thought out loud, since I didn't have my mind around the strangeness. And I didn't want to.

I just wanted to stay in the strangeness, since it made everything seem large and loud and quiet too. I couldn't find a way to say it that might not sound corny or just wrong. Harry took my hand. He was looking straight ahead and he started to hum. After a while he lifted my hand toward his face and he looked at it.

"Mannie, you have little monkey paws," he said. He held my hand as if it was a curious thing. Like it was an old bit of china washed up from a sunken ship. My hands have always had lots of wrinkles on them. Proves I'm an old soul, according to Eddie.

What I remember most is how the sky arched over us as if we were the only ones underneath it. We lay on our backs and watched the stars coming. You can't ever catch the moment when one pushes its tiny light through the black. It's just there. I had the feeling everything belonged to me. Not that I owned it, but that I was with it, an equal part, another element: me and the shaking trees, the puff of wind, the million tiny stars, the call of a bird passing over my skin, his hand around mine, Harry Jacob. I would have stayed just like that for a very long time, being a simple element in the world, but he turned on his side to face me.

I knew he was facing me.

He said my name. He said it as if it were a question. But he wasn't asking. He just looked right at me and he was close. I could feel his breath, or my name, in the tiny dark space between us. I could feel something else, like warmth coming from his body, but it wasn't exactly warmth, because it was getting inside me and buzzing, like a million bees passing through my pores.

Right at that moment I knew how Harry never had to worry about what life might want him to understand. Not like I did. Harry didn't look outward, he just let what he saw fall into his eyes. And now I was close enough to Harry that I could do it too. I turned toward him and I wanted to be closer still. The world around me was quiet; for once it didn't expect me to reply. I could almost feel the weight of his eyelids as they sank over his eyes. I said, "Harry, don't you want to kiss me now?" Because if he didn't kiss me I think I would have gone mad. I heard him laugh and then, just like that, his mouth came to mine and we were kissing, we definitely were.

And afterward I thought that was it: That was love. Love was life's secret purpose. I had been overcome in the most beautiful way possible. I could smell the air and I could feel Harry's arms around me. I could taste him.

I thought nothing bad could ever happen.

The next day Mum was gone.

chapter eighteen

Manon, my love, do you think of Eddie?" So there it was. Ivy said it. I knew she would.

Sometimes, only sometimes at home, someone might mention Eddie, but not like that, not directly, more just in passing, like, when Eddie did that, or that was Eddie's favorite, or there's that old friend of Eddie's. No one spoke directly of what had happened. But Ivy was different. Mum always said Ivy was overemotional.

I stared at the floor. I remembered Eddie and me sitting in Dad's Holden when we were just little. Eddie was in the driver's seat. He took the hand brake off and we rolled down the hill and crashed into the garage. He was making a *broom broom* noise the whole way. He was in heaven. He wasn't worried a bit.

The last time I saw him, he came into my room. He flopped on my bed and hassled me.

"So what's going on with you and Harry?" he said. I was reading. I kept the book close to my face and peered over it.

"Nothin'. Why?"

"'Cause it just looked like there was, at *Star Wars*." Eddie slipped out a suspicious-looking smile.

"Did Harry say there was?"

"Haven't spoken to him. Thought I'd ask you first."

"Nothing's happened," I lied. After all I hadn't had time to let it sink in myself, so I wasn't ready to spill any beans. The funny thing was that when I did tell someone about it, it wasn't Eddie and it wasn't Lucy either. "What made you think something was?"

Eddie looked up at the ceiling and considered. He didn't answer me.

"I reckon he fancies you." Eddie seemed pleased, almost triumphant, as if he knew more than I did. Or more than Harry even. He picked up the carved wooden bird that Harry had left and turned it over in his hand.

"Do you?" I pushed the book closer to my face in case I was blushing. But there wasn't any fooling Eddie. He pulled the book away and laughed.

"You're funny, Mannie. You're really funny," he said, and then he was chuckling and saying, "Imagine you and my mate Harry."

"Shut up, will you," I said, but he didn't; he got a lot of mileage out of it. He had to go and list all the great things about Harry Jacob, as if he was coaching me. He even told me what Harry liked and what Harry didn't like.

"He's not impressed by all that shit that those girls go on with, you know."

"What shit?"

"You know what I mean. He doesn't care who looks good and who doesn't and who's on the footy team, who's got money, who's cool. He doesn't even go to parties. You know what he likes?" Eddie laughed but not derisively. "Trees. He's got books about trees."

"Really?"

"Yeah. He doesn't like Skyhooks either, he likes music you wouldn't have heard of."

"How'd he hear it then?"

"From his brother. Same way you hear things."

"Very funny," I said, but I didn't care about the lecture because now that Eddie knew and appeared to be coaching me, it meant it was something. But then the phone was ringing and Eddie jumped up to get it. He just jumped off the bed and went out and then that was it.

I couldn't say anything to Ivy. I just kept looking at the floor.

"Oh, it's too sad," she cried. "Oh, my darling, there's been too much sadness in your young life."

Ivy drew me into her arms. I closed my eyes and rested my head

holding onto someone else

on Ivy's bony old shoulder. She was stroking my back, and rocking, just as if I were still a little girl. I tried not to let myself think of Eddie. I tried to hold my breath. And I stayed there with my wet eyes jammed up against Ivy, and Ivy didn't say a thing and neither did I.

chapter nineteen

Dad had held me in the same way. Rocking.

I remember it better than I remember any other thing that ever happened to me. It was four o'clock in the morning. I woke up because Dad was sitting on my bed. Just sitting there. So I knew straightaway that something wasn't right: for it to be so dark, for him to be sitting there in the black, crumpled and motionless, not leaving for work, not kissing me good-bye. How long had he been there?

"Dad?" I said. His hand went to hold mine.

"Something terrible has happened." His voice was wavering, thin, like a line of cotton. His dressing gown hung off him at an angle. I sat up. I braced myself. Then the words, so quietly wrenched out of my dad's throat, came at me, almost slowly, sailing out of the night, like the sparks from a distant explosion.

"Eddie's been killed."

I didn't cry, I broke: folded, like a snapped twig. I fell forward. I could hear myself screaming. My head was squashed into Dad's chest. My dad was gulping for air. I screamed into his flannel pajamas.

This is how it happened. Two policemen had come and knocked on the door at four o'clock in the morning. Dad must have heard them. He put his dressing gown on and walked through the dark house to open the door.

Eddie's death came into the house like a slow cold crack to a glass.

"Are you the father of Edouard Clarkeson? We're sorry, there's been an accident," said one of the policemen, taking off his hat in respect.

And then Dad coming to me, holding me, rocking.

Dad and I went to their bed. Mum was gone. Run off with Travis. We lay there while we waited for the day to come. Dad's hands gripped the blanket, he faced the ceiling. I could smell my mother next to me, could almost hear her sharp little breaths, but nothing seemed familiar, not Dad, not the bed, not the house, not the blank, blank hour we lay awake. Not even I was familiar to myself. There was nothing to hold on to. Not a single thing.

Dad got up out of the bed. He said, "I'm going to work." Then he fell against the wardrobe. His head was sideways, pressed into the door and he slid down the wardrobe as if his legs had just given in, like a man in a movie who had just been shot as he was about to climb a wall. He cried like a child. I didn't know what to do. I was supposed to be the child.

I said he couldn't go to work, it wasn't time yet. But there was nothing to do in the dark house.

Although I was waiting for it, I was dreading the daylight. Normal things would happen: There would be the dawn chorus of sparrows, John Jacob's motorbike growling down the road on the way to work, the warbly happy song of the magpies, someone taking a shower, the same man on the radio; milk, bells, the day arriving with its smell of toast and list of obligations, just as if it were normal, like every other day. Only it wasn't. The morning light was like a big lie that the world conspired to keep going.

But it came. The light came, just like every other morning, and Dad and I got dressed. We drove to Melbourne. To tell Mum. She came out to the car. We were sitting in it. She clutched a coat around her, frowning. She knew something was wrong, I could tell. It was as if she was expecting us. She leaned her head in the window where my dad was sitting. She didn't speak, she just stared at the violent silence on our faces. Then, as Dad said it, just as he said it to me, she folded up and her head dropped, but she didn't scream like I did. She just deflated, as if the life had gone from her. She sank to the ground.

Dad got out of the car and put his arms around her. There were tears dripping off his nose.

"It was the black ice," he said. She stared at him and gripped his arms, and then she started to breathe as if she was choking.

In winter, apart from the black ice, there was also frost. It killed the nasturtiums and the zucchini. It also killed lemon trees, unless you covered them up at night. In winter, when you woke up, everything outside was covered in ice. The skies were a pale gray, the grass was glittering in milky sheets and the trees turned scratchy and bare. When you walked Mou, your sneakers got wet in the frost and you always had to bring back some kindling. Dad poured his hot tea on the car windshield to get the ice off. Winter was so cold that when your feet touched the floor you'd have thought there was ice there too, but it was just the air cutting in through the cracks between the floorboards. We had slippers with sheep's wool on the inside, but still . . . The kitchen was the only room you could sit around in, because of the woodstove, which we had to keep going all day. In the morning, the water was frozen in the pipes and you had to remember to fill up the kettle the night before. In winter, the roads got the black ice on them.

They call it black ice. I don't know if it really is black. Maybe it is. All I know is you can't see it. It's deadly because it's not crunchy like the white frost; it's got no grip, no sound, no warning. The black ice is invisible and slippery and lurking. You can't tell if it's there or not.

It's where the shadows are, they say, where the sun can't reach. There are signs warning you to go slow, but you don't always do what signs tell you to do.

Eddie was driving, Harry was in the passenger seat. They were going to Melbourne. Eddie didn't have a seat belt on. He was careless like that. They said he died instantly.

Harry said it was his idea to go to Melbourne, but like I said, I didn't hold him responsible for what happened.

Mum came home with us. When we got back, there were two bunches of flowers waiting on the veranda. One was all forget-me-nots, with a pale blue bow. Already people knew. Soon people were coming over. Some brought pies. Mrs. Jacob sent over a basket of roses from her garden. The Bartholomews came, the Nelsons, the Hill family, and Eddie's friends came, various members of the footy team, the coach. . . . Lucy Brixton came with her mother, and they brought a beef stew. It's funny how any other time I would have been excited as hell to have all that food the people brought over, but you just don't get hungry when you're full up on sadness.

So, in the kitchen there was such a clutter of people and quiches and brandy that the awful silence in the house couldn't be heard. Dad was sometimes sunk in the couch, and Mou came to his lap. Mum seemed to appear and disappear, wandering through the house like a ghost. Harry's mum organized things, spoke to people, answered the phone, rang the priest. She gave me the job of finding vases for all the flowers that arrived, and writing thank-you letters for the kindness. Sometimes I would try to feel just the good feeling of gratitude and not the other bad feeling. I had sleeping tablets. At night, Dad sat on my bed till I went to sleep. I didn't want to be in my mind. It was like an unfamiliar, terrifying room with no one else in it. I didn't know it anymore. I was glad of the people filling up the house so that we wouldn't notice what was missing. At least not until the people went. Eddie's room, the outside bungalow, was left just as it was. No one moved his things or arranged them better.

Mum became very pale and quiet and she wouldn't eat at all. Most of the time there were tears in her eyes, which she kept wiping away with the back of her hand. Once she put her hand on my shoulder and patted me. I saw her staring at nothing.

Eddie's bungalow was like a museum. Each of us entered it, alone. We'd go there, one by one, sometimes passing each other, looking away, as if we'd been caught. Caught just looking at Eddie's things, his emptied things. You had to do it, to stand there and slowly let the emptied bed, the ghost-cold stillness in the room, convince you that he had gone. Yes, he is gone. Yes, he is not here. Yes, something has finished.

His corduroy jacket hung over the back of his chair; thrown on top of it, a red shirt. His bed was unmade. I stood in the room and looked. Sometimes I picked something up and then I put it back. That old red shirt thrown over the back of the chair, a thing I'd never looked at before but had always seen on Eddie. It was just a shirt, but

I kept holding it, pressing it to my face, inhaling it. It wasn't a shirt anymore, it was a last, uncareful gesture. And then it was an absence. Eddie had gone from it.

I saw Mum in there. She was sitting on Eddie's bed, a piece of paper in her hand. Her dark hair hung in a plait down her back. She looked like a child woken from a bad dream.

"What's that?" I asked. Mum looked up, red-eyed and distant.

"I don't know. Something of Eddie's." I knew what she was looking at. I'd seen everything in the room. It was a piece of paper with some words Eddie had scribbled on it. There was an address and then the words "D. Wolton," and beneath that: "It is Sunday. Outside the wind . . . She's bitten by the wind again." That was all it said. It was just a fragment, a sign of life, a last word. But you couldn't help looking for a clue, a reason why. Why had it happened? Grief makes you so unreasonable.

"You all right?" I said.

She didn't answer. She hung her head down. Like her neck was broken. My heart curled inward.

"I'm living the wrong life, Manon. It's a mistake." She closed her eyes and put her head in her hands. "I'm sorry. I'm so sorry."

In the impermanence of life, it was impossible to accept the for-everness of death. When something is suddenly wrenched from you, you stumble after it, stunned and aching, loss leading you to the abyss, where you hover like a vagrant, forever wanting that thing to come back, perhaps straining to see it and call it back. It's a common lament: Oh, my child come back to me, Oh, lover come back to me, Oh, my friend come back to me, Oh, Eddie come back.

Let me tell you, the lonely infinity of memory was a wretched place to live, and I was getting out.

chapter twenty

"Manon, dear, and how's your father? Is he coping?" Ivy held my hands on her lap.

"I don't know. He doesn't say." I sniffed.

"Don't you two talk?" she cried. "Oh, you must. You should talk to your father. You're together in this."

I couldn't explain to Ivy but Dad just never seemed to have anything to say anymore. We were both changed. It was as if the life we had before had gone, as if a big warm blanket had been yanked off us and we were adjusting to the cold in our own separate ways. My way was to want and want, to want Eddie back. Dad's way was to give up on people altogether. All he invested his energy in now was the animals. A dog will never desert you, that's for sure. Besides, Dad was tired, and when he did come home he only seemed to hover there. He hovered in the hall, holding his bag with one hand and with the other picking up the letters on the table and staring at them a while, turning them over but not opening them. That was how he appeared in my mind's eye, like a passenger caught in transit. A passenger. I almost repeated the word out loud as it came to me with such a satisfying ring of accuracy. When Dad came home from work, he sank into the almost-new couch in the living room as if he was never going to get up out of it again. With his squawky old pale face, he looked wrong on the buoyant cherry couch; he was like a dirty gray stick caught on the edge of a sumptuous ball gown. He bent his head close to Mou, and then he lay back with his eyes half closed and his hand, a tired old claw, lying on the dog's head. He patted every now and then, and said dog things to Mou. This was enough. Just this simple mild thing of sitting and patting the dog was enough for Dad.

"You should let Mou get up," I said. Now that Mum was gone again, what did we care if the couch got dirtied up a bit? Dad nodded wearily. He'd smile at me, but it was such a worn-out old smile, and everything he said was exactly the same. He was just opening his mouth and letting out the suite of suitable sentences that lay stacked on top of each other.

"How was your day, Mannie?"

"Okay."

"What shall we do about dinner? Did you remember to lock up the chickens?"

"Yeah." I walked to the fridge and removed a box of fish fingers from the freezer.

"Has Mou had a walk?" he called from the couch. He knew I walked Mou every afternoon, up to the Nelsons' orchards and sometimes to Wally's dam. But still he asked and still I told him yes. Yes, the chickens are in and Mou's been walked. He nodded, but only because it was his habit. It was because he worked with sick animals all day long that he had forgotten how to inquire about what went on in a person's mind. He only knew about snake bites and flyblown sheep and the wounds that came up, ugly and blaring, on an animal's body. He didn't think about a person's heart, about my heart, or even his own, for that matter, not anymore. Dad's heart was worn down like an old carpet, with the light and the smells and the music moving over him in a familiar way. He just let it happen, let the days pile up on top of him.

I didn't have to let that happen to me. I was just going to waste. That was how I felt. Like that bunch of wild flag irises stuck in a jar of water and left on the bench next to the toaster and the fruit bowl. Like just another thing that sits there, losing petals, dropping crumbs.

I told Ivy my plans. I told her I was going to Paris. She nodded at me, but she didn't say anything about the money. So I had to ask.

"Ivy. Eddie told me that there was money put away for us. He said we were allowed to have it when we were eighteen. Money Benjamin put away."

"Oh," said Ivy and she frowned. "I don't know. I remember something like that. Didn't you speak to your father about it? He'd know."

"No. I didn't ask him." I didn't want to tell Ivy I'd gone without telling Dad. How could I tell him I was leaving? I couldn't face it, to tell you the truth. I couldn't face leaving him alone, but I couldn't stay just for his sake either. What would Ivy think of me if she knew I'd just deserted my dad? She'd think I was like Mum. Selfish. A deserter. I heaved a big sigh.

"There's a lawyer, though," she said. "He might know. Mr. Crock. You could look him up. He works in the city. He looks after all Benjamin's affairs. He pays my bills here. He's . . ." She waved with her hand toward something in the room and then she closed her eyes as if trying to remember.

"Don't worry, Ivy," I said. I could tell she was tired. Her eyes stayed closed for a while. I didn't want to go see that lawyer, anyway. I had other plans, more pressing. For some reason I couldn't think past that day. I didn't want to. It was like looking into a hole when you can't see the bottom. You feel disoriented. I had to keep my attention fixed on the tiny distance ahead of me, not the large one.

"Dear, it's our lunchtime. Will you come back again?" said Ivy. A bell was ringing.

"Of course. I'll come back tomorrow," I said. I gave Ivy a big hug and I was careful not to squeeze too hard, since she seemed brittle as a paper nautilus.

I really intended to go back again the next day, and if the next day had gone as I planned, I would have gone back. But it didn't. It certainly didn't.

chapter twenty-one

The next place I had to go was the other side of town.

3/37 Tennyson St., St. Kilda. D. Wolton. It is Sunday. Outside the wind . . . She's bitten by the wind again.

I had that bit of paper with Eddie's writing on it. It had been making a lump in my brain, that bit of paper. It was giving me a notion. I only let it out every now and then. Who was the girl in the wind? I see myself knocking on a door, number three. I see the door opening and there is a girl. D. Wolton. Her name is Demeter, or Delia. She is mythic. She has long white hair, like Lucy, only she is beautiful in that Sleeping Beauty way. Soft and fine and gentle, like mist. She knows who I am immediately. She has this way of knowing. "Manon," she says, almost in a whisper. "We've been waiting for you." And she leads me inside. . . .

Don't get me wrong. I knew Eddie was dead. But there was something of him there, behind that door. There had to be something more; even just a new knowing was something. Sometimes I accidentally saw Eddie, for the tiniest moment. It was as if a speck of him had surfaced in someone else. Maybe it was just a curve of dark hair falling over a forehead, but it made me jump. And afterward I'd sink a bit.

I didn't know if I could go there straightaway. I'd been thinking and thinking about it for a long while. I'd been building up to it. I was counting on it, somehow, and now that it was within reach I started to panic. Besides, I was all emotional after seeing Ivy, and I had to dry out a bit and build up again. I decided I'd go lurk around the area for a while, get myself more prepared.

It took me over an hour to get to St. Kilda. It's a beach suburb. Once it was grand, with lots of old fancy apartment buildings with swirly columns and bay windows. Then it went under and the immigrants moved in and opened cake shops, and artists moved in since it was cheap. Now there are lots of places selling sex, and there's housing for hobos, and great old crumbling white hotels with dirty carpets where you can see punk bands. When we were kids we sometimes went ice skating there at St. Moritz, but the whole rink got burned down and they're going to build a hotel there instead.

The best thing about St. Kilda is the mad face at Luna Park. The mouth is open and that's what you walk through. The eyes are wide and frenzied and there is a row of colored lightbulbs and the lips are bared so you can see teeth. So it's crazed, but also old and rickety, fenced in by the shaky wood lattice of the roller coaster. It looms, leers, and creaks there in the center of St. Kilda, like a resident ghost, like a memory from a past that won't go away and won't come forward either. It's like the corner of your mind that itches, the small madness that you live with simply because it won't go away. You cover it in new clothes, you cage it up inside your strong chest, but still, it is there.

I went to the beach. I locked up my bike and went and sat on the beach. The sand was white and puckered and full of puddles of sun and cigarette stubs. There was a German couple sitting next to me on a bench. They had sensible sandals on, and money belts. The German woman had an unfortunate face. Unfortunate because it wasn't the kind of face that you'd want to wake up next to. It might make you feel as if you were being examined for some untidiness, studded, as it was, with poky eyes. I felt bad for having such a mean thought, so I smiled kindly at the couple. They received my smile with an awkward uncertainty.

To tell you the truth, I wasn't feeling that good. Not as good as I was meant to be feeling. Not how I'd planned to feel. At least that German couple, bad mornings or not, had each other. Most people were sitting in clumps or strolling along in pairs. They were together.

When no one understands you, you go to great lengths to understand yourself. You have conversations, inward ones. Only problem is, the person I talk to inside my head is very mean. What the mean person said right then was: Do you ever see yourself in the mirror and think you are the ugliest person in the world? I nodded, and banged the sand out flat with the palm of my hand. I certainly wasn't a very pretty person. Mean Person was always reminding me of things like that, always saying: See, you're so hopeless. Now look how selfish you are. Or, Boy, you're a bad kind of fish. Sometimes I imagined what a kind person would say, but the thing was, you couldn't believe it since you knew it would just be fake reassurances, patting your leg, not discriminating. And if there was a wise person, well, she was very reclusive. So that left Mean Person hogging the conversations. It was Mean Person who was responsible for me having mean thoughts about German tourists. It wasn't me.

I stared out at the sea. A small ship crawled along the horizon. I lay back and closed my eyes.

The day of the funeral, Dad and I went to see Harry in the hospital. Mum wouldn't come. I would have preferred to go alone, but I couldn't tell them that. Harry lay on a bed covered in a white sheet. He was behind a gray screen that crinkled in and out like an accordion. He had tubes coming out of his nose and wrist. His left eye was just a slit surrounded by purple puffed-up skin. There was a bandage around his jaw. He was staring at the ceiling when we came in. His head turned toward us. He didn't smile. His busted-up face was full of sadness. Dad and I were all dressed up for the funeral. Dad's tie was crooked. I was wearing Mum's flared skirt with a shirt tucked in. None of us looked like we normally looked. Harry, all hurt, flattened, bare brave arms pinned down by tubes; us, formal and dark and stiff. We stood there; he lay there. Tears rolled down his face. I'd never seen him look like that before. I'd never seen him crushed by anything.

"You all right, Harry?" said Dad.

Harry nodded and I went close to the bed. Harry's slopey eyes followed me. I took his hand and Dad put his arm around me and we all had tears dribbling down our faces and no one could say anything that those dribbling tears weren't already saying. We were all feeling, not for ourselves, but for each other, because someone else's pain is so very hard to take, even harder than your own. It was as if we made a circle, the three of us, and inside the circle, sadness welled up and ebbed between us like an echo in a cave. Our hearts linked up, like injured arms holding together against a huge, unstoppable tide. They held a place to pour into.

"What do they say's wrong with you, Harry?" said my dad. Harry shifted as if he had to locate that part of himself.

"Mainly internal damage. Crushed ribs, punctured spleen."

"Are you in pain?" I asked.

"I'm all right," he said, but I could tell it was painful. I looked at his wrist, the white skin.

It was hard to locate the other feelings I'd had for Harry, the love feelings. It was like trying to remember a tune when you'd become deaf. A sudden rip in time had happened and there was a then and there was a now, and they'd been wrenched so far apart I couldn't make the two meet up. Anyway, I told myself there was only so much feeling you could do all at once, and love and grief were both about the biggest things you could feel, and the two just couldn't fit in one small body at the same time, so love would have to wait.

I didn't go back to see Harry in the hospital, though. It was too hard and sad and strained, and I couldn't go through it. I didn't see him again, not until he got out.

chapter twenty-two

I must have drifted off to sleep on the beach. When I woke up it was late in the afternoon. I'd had a bad dream about an injured bird. I'd rushed around holding it, asking the people in clumps and pairs on the beach to help me save the bird. But no one would.

I got up, brushed the sand off my cheek, and went in search of food.

Je suis un clapot, je suis un clapot. I was making it a little tune in my head. *I am a toad, I am a toad.* It didn't sound the same in English. *Clapot* wasn't a real word. It came from me mispronouncing the French word for *toad* when I was a kid, and Eddie ran with it. I liked the word, liked the shape of it coming out of my mouth. It became a secret insult Eddie and I slung at each other. *T'es un clapot, toi!* I would whisper at him (if I was feeling very French). Or he'd just yell it out at me, if he saw me at school or walking home. *Hey, Clapot!*

Whenever I felt bad about something, I said to myself, "But I'm lucky I'm me and not Diedre Disaster." Diedre was a girl at school whose legs were so white you could see the veins zigzagging behind the skin. It was a crime to have legs that white. So it would have been bad to have been Diedre. I said it quietly so that God wouldn't hear. I had a feeling it wasn't a generous sentiment. I said it then, but already it seemed to have lost its effect. After all, I couldn't be sure anymore that it might not have been better to be Diedre Disaster. Maybe she never lost anyone, maybe she was about to find her thing: She would blossom, marry a furniture-maker with kind hands, roast a chicken, and live in an honest white house on Hope Street.

I wandered into a music shop. I thought I'd get a present for Ivy. A Fats Waller record or Louis Armstrong or something old-time and happy. I went up to the counter and waited while the boy behind it served someone else. He was a tall boy with funny peaked eyebrows and hair that stood out at different angles. The girl he was serving was young and stood like a shrub, quiet and spreading and needing sunlight. She had soft white cheeks, a moon face, and a lot of black clothes that wafted around her like a storm cloud. She looked up at him with her eyes but not her face; she kept her face looking down. He slid the record over the counter in a brown paper bag with the receipt lying on top. She stood still a moment then pulled the record out of the bag and pushed it back toward him.

"Could you sign it?" she asked, looking at him directly this time. Her face was wide and blushing, but her eyes were squinting as if the boy behind the counter was a bright light flaring down at her. The bright light nodded and grabbed a pen from underneath the counter. But he hardly even bothered to smile at her. It was mean of him not to smile. If it was me, I would have beamed.

"Who to?" he asked. He didn't need to smile; the girl loved him anyway.

"To Corinne." Her feet crossed and uncrossed beneath her. She leaned into the counter and watched him sign.

"There you go," he said, pushing it back toward her. She turned it around to face her and she read it, her face showing neither pleasure nor displeasure, just a fierce concentration, as if she were looking at a map of Los Angeles and trying to find a street that didn't really exist. She muttered her thanks and pushed the record into her bag, moving quickly as if it was urgent now that she should leave. He didn't even watch her go. He turned to me.

"Need any help?" he said, raising those peaky eyebrows. He seemed brusque, almost bored and impatient with life. His foot tapped away maniacally beneath the counter, and he rubbed his hair so it stood up even more.

"Got any Fats Waller?" I acted nonchalant.

He bunched up his lips and looked at me with a bored kind of frown. It was as if I'd asked him a supremely dull question. I worried for a minute that I still had sand on my cheek, or maybe I really was the ugliest person in the world.

"In the jazz section." His voice sounded tired. I could tell

immediately that the jazz section was the wrong section to be looking in, in his opinion, and if I'd wanted to impress him I'd just lost a
lot of marks. I went and looked, but I wasn't concentrating very well
on looking. Why would I want to impress him, anyway? I wondered
if he was famous.

"You in a band?" I asked when I went back to the counter with
The Best of Fats Waller in my hand.

"Yep."

"What's it called?"

"The Thin Captains." His fingers rapped on the counter. He
leaned on one arm and his eyes seemed to swagger, like a drunk looking for a fight.

"What do you play?"

I wasn't quite sure what he was thinking. He appeared to be
examining me. I felt my hand floating up to my shoulder and I
pushed my fingers under the strap of my dress. He stood up straight.
He was good-looking. I realized it all of a sudden and I felt strange
and loaded up with the realization.

"I'm the singer," he said. I didn't reply. Instead I looked above him
at a poster, because I could tell my heart was behaving strangely,
clawing at my chest like a yabbie in a bucket. "We're playing tonight.
At the Espy. Come along, if you want." He reached underneath the
counter and pulled out a flyer. I took it and glanced up at him. It was
meant to be a casual glance but it didn't come out casual. It came out

burning. I could feel my eyes opening out and trying to swallow the sense of him. His mouth moved a little bit on one side. He wouldn't be swallowed, not by my eyes.

"Okay," I said and then, just to make myself not appear too available, I added, "I'll try."

He shrugged and I felt my cheeks reddening, as if all that strange flapping and leaping inside had whooshed up into my face. I put my hand over my mouth and stopped for a minute. He was still looking at me, but I couldn't think of a thing to say, so I had to leave. There was no other choice.

Once I was a safe distance away from the shop, I examined the flyer. It didn't tell me anything more about him, the Thin Captain. It did say Esplanade Hotel, Gershwin Room, five dollars cover charge, St. Kilda. So then I knew what I would do that night. I walked up the road, but my eyes had gone soft and I wasn't noticing anything. I was creating a dream. The Thin Captain was singing and even though there was a crowd of people watching, I knew it was a song for me. This little fantasy was every now and then disturbed by the memory of what went on between us in the shop. Nothing, said Mean Person. He hardly noticed you. Then again, I thought cheerfully, he did ask me to come tonight and he didn't ask the black-clad girl. It was especially pertinent, this last observation, that he hadn't asked the other girl. I clung to it. Proof that I was especially invited. Then I fell back to dreaming of the Gershwin Room, where it would all happen.

The thing about Harry, I thought, as I saw him in my mind's eye, standing there forlornly in the crowd at the Gershwin room, was that he didn't do anything. Not anything you could really be proud of or boast about. If someone said to you, "And what does your husband do?" and just say Harry Jacob was your husband, well, you'd have nothing very impressive to say. "Oh, he picks apples and fixes things around the house, and he whistles."

It was true that Harry was just a big slowcoach. He was always stopping and cocking his head and listening. "Hear that?" he said when we walked down by the Springs. "I reckon it's a skylark." I couldn't tell how the sound came into his head, right when we were talking or walking along and I was so caught up in the thoughts I was having I couldn't hear anything, because I wasn't listening. Why would you always listen to the big blur of buzzing and trilling and cracking and croaking that came out of the bush and paddocks? The other annoying thing Harry did was to stop when a dog came along, any old dog, and Harry had to have a pat. And not only dogs, also flowers, most particularly roses. I didn't mind him patting and sniffing and touching; it was just that he was always stopping and it made me feel as if he wasn't ever getting anywhere, because he was too distracted. I bet that Thin Captain never stopped to smell plants and flowers and apple blossoms. That Thin Captain was going places.

· · · · ·

By the time Harry got out of the hospital, I already knew I was leaving. I was leaving Blackjack Road and I was leaving my old life. The problem with Harry was that he may have suited the old Mannie, but he wouldn't suit the new one. Like my mum said, he was just a country boy. It was because of Harry that Eddie had been driving to Melbourne. Harry said they were going to see a band that he wanted to see. I didn't blame him for the accident. I really didn't. It wasn't that. It was just I got this idea that he wasn't right.

He came over to see me when he got out of the hospital. He stood in the doorway holding a bunch of blue hydrangeas.

He pushed them toward me. "Thanks," I said. They dripped all over me. I went to the kitchen and found a vase. In the living room, Harry sat on the couch and I stood by the fire. Harry didn't look right on the new couch. He hovered on the edge of it, his hands clasped in front of him. He had lovely hands, though. I didn't let myself look at his lovely hands. I knew I should have sat down next to him and we should have been close, but I was afraid to sit near him in case it made me love him. So I stood and I rocked on my feet and I tried to think of something to say.

"You fully recovered, Harry? Your ribs and internals, I mean."

"Yeah, as good as. I have to take it easy for a while."

I nodded slowly. I didn't know what else to say.

"You seem different, Mannie," he said.

"I am different." I shrugged. "Aren't you?"

"Yeah. Kind of. Are you okay?"

"Yeah. I just don't feel —" I looked at the floor. Harry stood up.

"I understand, Mannie. It's fine. I'll go." He put his hand on my shoulder and I looked at him and saw his slopey-down eyes looking so soft I almost cried. I almost bled. I almost fell toward him. But I was kind of stunned and frozen too. It confounded me, how my feelings jumped one way and then, just as strong, they could jump the other way. How could I trust them? I couldn't. I stuffed them inside and stood all stiff as a cold fish. I'd made my decision. I should stick to what I knew. Harry's hand trailed away down my arm as he left. I felt terrible afterward, and I went and cried.

I was right not to fall back into the arms of Harry Jacob. Harry just wouldn't suit the new A-class Mannie. Not like the Thin Captain would. I walked farther up the street. I just walked because I was in the kind of spectacular mood that I was meant to be in. My situation had finally found me, I was sure of it. The more I thought about what had happened in the music shop, the more I was sure, and the more I felt sure, the more everything began to change around me. I was in love. What a relief. The address, Eddie's address, began its burning again, and I was beginning to feel sure about that too. All in all, I was pretty convincing.

It was like the beginning of summer when hot air wafts in the window: There was an excited bursting feeling inside me. But it couldn't quite burst; there was a tightness inside me too. And the bursting was pushing up against the tightness and the tightness was pushing back against the bursting and this created a supremely good and giddy pressure, an almost almost feeling, more almost than I'd ever before been. There was, if I let myself admit it, a little sharp edge to the feeling. If I could have, I would have kept the almost almost feeling and not risked its ending. I truly considered never going to see the Thin Captain, and just feeding my heart with the idea of him, crumb by crumb, so I could live forever in a permanent state of almost almost. It might not work out like it should, if I did go. Maybe I didn't need to go to number 37 Tennyson Street either. But I knew I had to do both, because the minute I thought of not going, the almost almost feeling began to deflate and lose pressure. So I quickly pumped it up again by assuring myself that I would go.

I did try at least to stop thinking of the Thin Captain, but he was everywhere. He was in the blue sky beating down on my bare shoulders, he was in the fancy old flats, he was in my future. I tried to think of a song to sing, but the only song that kept coming to me was a Bob Dylan song that Harry used to sing, and I wasn't going to sing that.

I put myself back on track and looked for a place to eat. I was on Fitzroy Street, which was lined with shops, two big old hotels, and a lot of Italian restaurants. I went into one that seemed kind of old and unpopular. I felt sorry for it. An old couple was seated with their backs against the wall and they were both just looking out. They weren't speaking. When I walked in, the man stood up and stretched his big belly forward. He came toward me.

"Can I get some pasta or something?" I said. (It was way past lunchtime.) He turned and looked at the woman and she nodded.

"You want a pasta Napoli?" he said.

"Sure."

I figured the old Italian couple had run out of things to say to each other. I worried about that. To tell you the truth, I was worried about ending up with a husband. I was worried that I'd soon get tired of him. Once I'd heard all his opinions and stories, then what? Couples must just stop having conversations after a while — conversations that sweep you up and make you bleed or bend or fizz up and blur the lines. You only get dribbly little insipid moments of speech about the nice soup, or the poppy seed you've got stuck between your teeth. This was what I'd thought about me and Harry Jacob. What if it got boring? I imagined the kind of conversations a couple like me and Harry might end up having. It went like this:

"Do you like it?" says she.

"What?" says he.

"Do you like the soup? I put chili in it," says she.

"Yeah. It's nice." He puffs on it and scoops some up in a spoon and wonders, what next? What's after dinner?

She notices he has spilled some soup on his jumper. She feels slightly irritated and reaches for the salt.

"Hey, darling, how old you think I am? Huh?" said the old man as he plunked a bowl of pasta in front of me.

"Fifty."

"Sixty-three." He thumped his chest triumphantly and laughed.

chapter twenty-three

I left the restaurant and walked along the street, thinking of the concert and the Thin Captain and the rightness of it all. I was rolling out. I wasn't even limping a bit. Actually, I was feeling like a cat. I was all kind of luxurious and nonchalant; I was made of satin. I was slinky and smoothed out and nothing could get a grip on me, nothing.

I was slipping up against the night with my burning big heart, like a happy singing boy. It was as if something had arrived inside me, the way a letter slips inside a letterbox, only it wasn't a letter, it was a glorious new knowing, a revelation, and it belonged entirely to that moment. It may sound obvious, but what I knew only in that moment, and never in the same way since, was simply that nothing mattered. I knew it then, and so it was true then. Simple as that. I could just keep wandering and it wouldn't even matter where I went. I was just a slip of air, shaped like a girl.

Usually everything mattered so much.

There was a small boy in a red shirt and shorts walking too. He was chubby and his shirt was tucked in. I watched him throw a stone fiercely at a group of pigeons on the pavement. The pigeons burst into the air, fluttering up like an explosion. The boy walked on, pushing a red Popsicle in his mouth, little sausage arms swinging triumphantly.

I found a beautiful yellowed ginkgo leaf and pinned it in my hair, but it broke a little. I had half this beautiful leaf in my hair, and the sky was glowing like a pumpkin, so I was feeling special. The lights of bars and cafés were painting the night like an invitation. I was wanting to say "yes." A tall dark gypsy woman stood by a table on the street. She charged a dollar for a question. She had something that glittered. She definitely did. There were little gold disks sewn on her butter-colored scarf to make the glittering, and she wore a long swishing skirt. For my question I asked about love, but I didn't necessarily plan to believe her. I just wanted the thing that glittered, the way of belonging to the low night street.

The gypsy woman took my hand. She said, "You are blessed with luck, you will always be protected. Are you an artist?" I shook my head. "Your heart," she said, "is well-linked to your mind. You must honor both, but you must stop loving the dangerous man, you must love the family man."

I wanted to ask her how you can tell who is dangerous and who is a family man, but I'd only paid for one question. Anyway, I thought, a family can be a dangerous thing to have.

There was an old man pushing a big stack of plastic rubbish bags on a trolley. He was wearing white sneakers and a brown suit. He looked tired and the bags were gleaming in an evil way. I knew the city had a dark gray heart. The buildings were porous and hungry, standing so close and narrow. Life had smudged its dirt and love all over the inside and the outside of them. You got the feeling that every corner was alive and beating and curious. You'd only have to look at it, to press your heart into it, and it could pound right back at you.

There was a poster on a wall, half ripped up, with a great word written on it. DER FENSTERPUTZER. I figured from the picture that it meant "window washer" in German.

Der Fensterputzer.

Der Fensterputzer.

Vroom vroom.

There was an old yellow dog waiting outside the supermarket. I got close to him, I got close and stayed with him a while. He had a worried look, so I was whispering to him. I was saying, "See, you don't have to worry, nothing matters." The yellow dog didn't seem convinced, so I changed tack. I tried philosophy. I said, "Imagine how much worse it would be if everything was known, if everything was clear and reasonable like the red plastic clock in our kitchen? Just think how that clock must wish it could improvise, or make a guess, or lie in the sun with not a plan in the world."

The yellow dog suddenly wagged its tail and stood up, and I was just thinking that dogs were the most philosophical beings in the world when I saw that he was wagging at a girl, not my philosophy.

The girl was bright and brimming with blondness. They were a good pair, she and the yellow dog, both large and pedigreed. She was wearing a mini and a pink boobtube that said DISCO QUEEN, so she was naturally showing a lot of the kind of skin that tanned people have. It was top-notch skin: skin that looked like polished pinewood furniture. I stood up as she untied the dog. Pedigree, I thought to myself again, that's what she has, because of the strong legs and swinging ponytail. And just as I was forming the word in my mind, the disco queen smiled at me and said hi. She said it so nicely that I felt immediately ashamed of myself for thinking pedigree, and I tried to make up for it by smiling like an angel. She didn't seem to notice either way, and you could tell life was easy for her. She and her dog bounced off in their good yellow glow. "I'm not a bad person," I said to myself. "I've simply come out of left field. I'm a stray and, anyway, whatever I am, I'm not it yet. I'm still becoming." In fact, I'd always believed that I was once a horse, because I loved to run down a hill. And Eddie was a fish. He was a swaggerer, if you know what I mean. Flimsy but lovable.

Oh, the piece of dark summer sky; it told nothing.

I walked off in the same direction as the yellow pair. I don't know why, I just did.

Pedigree Disco Girl went into a takeaway chicken shop. I hid in a nearby bookshop and waited for her to come out. She took an awfully long time, and I was beginning to think she possibly wasn't an exciting enough prospect. It wasn't that I was interested in Pedigree Disco Girl, it was just that I was in the mood to live someone else's life. Someone's easy life. I figured that you couldn't possibly make mistakes when you're following someone else's path. Even better, you wouldn't have to make a single decision. Maybe you could even learn through imitation, how to live easy. It was an experiment in being a dog. Dogs just go along without doubting a thing.

I picked up a book so as not to look suspicious. It was a large book with a dark painting on the front. Inside, it was full of paintings, mostly of the ocean or a river at night. I was just looking casually, noticing the paintings, when a strange thing began to happen. It happened slowly and deeply and almost mysteriously.

First the paintings started to look back at me. They were getting me involved. They were stirring me up. There wasn't much in them: the odd eerie blues, the smoky night sky and the body of water lying large and gentle, and the sense of something else, a boat or a figure, or the light of some distant land, a bridge. But none of this was clear; it was as if it had been painted with mist or darkness or music, not paint. And it was this vagueness that called to me, because it was soft and possible, and there was room for you within it. Nothing was distinct or outlined in the painting, as if nothing really had a certain place at all, and somehow this seemed true, and the truth of it wasn't intended, but only hummed, only there in a blurred and hovering way, only there like a sad distant melody. I guess what I saw in the paintings wasn't something you could see with your eyes. It was some other part of me that was seeing it. It was like music, how you hear it through your ears, but somewhere else in you receives it. I was getting the soft singing of those pictures; they were singing my own heart's song. I knew that mist around me and I felt myself standing in it, just being there, like a lamp in a dark room. Maybe you need the darkness deep around you, just to show you how to find your own light.

I was so overcome with that soft mist, and the me inside it, that I completely forgot Pedigree Girl and my brief life as a dog. I just wanted to keep the book, wanted to be able to look at those paintings always. The price was almost as much as the horse money, and I thought how people would think I was mad to spend thirty-five dollars on a book. If I bought it there'd be no money left for accommodation, but I wasn't feeling like I needed a bed as much as I needed those paintings. I was approaching the counter even as I argued with myself, so I knew I was going to buy it anyway. Even if I found reasons not to, I still would. I felt guilty and giddy all at once, and smelled the book a couple of times before they put it in a bag. It was the very first book I had ever bought for myself. I told myself I'd done a good thing, I'd bought something that would last. The book was better than the silver shoes.

I put the book in my backpack and walked along the footpath that wound by the beach and led to the Esplanade Hotel. I was in that special cat-mood again, and I felt inspired in an uncertain way. I walked past Luna Park and it didn't let out one single snort.

"Good sign, Mannie," I said to myself, in a plucky way. I was back on track. The book had done it. I let the sky fill my head with its large ideas.

I almost didn't want to get there, because it's so much more fun when you're on the way. But before I could stop it, the Esplanade Hotel loomed in front of me, white and grand but also shabby, like a big white-toothed grin with fillings. There was a spreading stairway leading inside and red swirly carpet that looked like internal organs. I stood a while and an odd clutch of thoughts came into my mind that had nothing to do with the course of events so far. I remembered how once I had dyed my hair black, but it only made me look worse and the dye stained my fingers.

I went directly to the bar and ordered a red wine. I didn't like standing on the carpet of internal organs, so I sat on a stool. It was only eight o'clock. That meant I'd be there for three hours before the band came on. At least I could see out the big windows. The sun hovered over the horizon like a huge luminous plate, the color of red coals. Around it the sky was doused in pink. People were watching it, stopping to comment, saying, "Look how beautiful," and then wondering how best to fit such beauty into a size that they could use, how to tuck it into their hearts or add it to their store of significant observations. Sailors on the large boats that lumbered along the horizon were probably leaning on their mops, remembering who they'd sailed away from: a sad-eyed girl; a stooped, sweet-smelling mother; a batch of sleeping children. A sunset is like autumn in that way. It's the sinking away of light. It makes you take hold of a feeling and rock it in your arms, as if otherwise it might diffuse into the long stretch of past that falls like a dark shadow behind you. I met a lot of people while I sat there. Because of my dress, I suppose. There was this pudgy solitary lady, who was slightly balding, in a red tracksuit. She had a bag of green beans and a sensitivity to chemicals. She was sitting at the other end of the bar but she kept edging closer and asking me questions. Her name was Ellen and she complained a lot. She said, "Have you ever seen an okapi?" I said, "What's an okapi?" She said it was an animal with big ears that lived in America. "I've never been to America," I said. "Well, I have and it was terrible," she said. I wished she hadn't come so close; I was getting intolerant again. Next, she wanted to know why I was drinking alone.

" 'Cause I've had a hard life," I said, slouching down close to the bar, like a bitter old tough guy.

"Ha!" She laughed and thumped her fist on the bar. "Who hasn't? Don't think you're so special." Already I was thinking Ellen was sour. She was shriveling my air. Worse than that, maybe she had a point. There was this old guy with baggy blue eyes but I could tell he wasn't about to involve himself, so out of desperation I said, "Hey, what's your name?"

"Clarence," he said.

"You ever been to America, Clarence?" said Ellen.

"Nuh. But I used to drive tractors."

167

"Tractors!" screeched Ellen. "What's that got to do with anything?" I sighed and said I wished I could drive a tractor, which was a big friendly lie. I never once in my life felt the urge to drive a tractor, but I wanted to say something encouraging to Clarence since I felt responsible for dragging him into Ellen's sour orbit. Clarence, I could tell, was another one of those happy people. I was watching him the way I'd watched Pedigree Girl, to see how he did it. But he was just drinking beer.

Two workmen came along and stood leaning on the bar next to us. One of the workmen started talking about a documentary he'd watched on television the night before. It was about Cézanne. I said, "Hey, I'm gonna study art." I was thinking of my new book, *Nocturne*. Suddenly I fancied myself as an artist, but as soon as I said it I felt like a big faker again, so I tried to frown the faking away. The workman didn't even notice that I was showing off. He just raised his eyebrows and said, "Are ya just? Well, did you know them paintings were a sexual thing?"

I asked him how. "How were they sexual?"

He said, "The mountains, they were breasts." He didn't turn or lift his head at all. He was holding a pot of beer in one hand, and with the other he made the shape of a breast in the air.

"What utter bullshit!" said Ellen, and she stood up and grabbed her green beans and walked away. I didn't care that she'd gone. I was worrying that art was more complex than I thought, and maybe I wasn't going to be an artist after all.

There was a man in the corner laughing. Harvey. He looked like he was growing there, actually. He was a man with a wide flat nose, and his eyes were just two dark moons disappearing behind a great mound of cheek. His body, large, round, and motionless, lost beneath the years of sitting still, one hand continually reaching for chips, the other holding a glass of beer. He looked to me as if he were holding his arms to the world: giant, soft, fat arms that expected nothing, just to go on without stopping, without starting. I would have liked to be still enough to enter Harvey's softly continuous world, a rolling-on-and-on kind of world, which would keep holding him on his bar stool, while one hand reached like a lever for chips. He said he lived in a boardinghouse in St. Kilda.

"They're gonna go. Developers," said the workman who'd made the breast in the air. He was referring to boardinghouses. "We just made some into apartments." He bought me another wine. I accepted it since he was just being neighborly. I was feeling woozy. I was thinking about what I didn't know:

To be a blade of grass.

To have a position in the world.

To be still.

The word for apple in Spanish.

The length of time it would take Manon Clarkeson to become a tree.

How I'd lived so long without becoming a certain shape.

"The big question," said Clarence, the happy man, "is whether they're going to be able to sell it, anyway." He was talking about the pub. There were developers wanting to put slot machines in it. Harvey was against it. The workmen didn't seem to care.

The big question, I thought to myself, so as not to lessen the importance of Clarence's big question, was whether you are able to say yes. There was always a tiny adventure waiting for you. Between the beginning and the end, between one pair of arms and another . . . Between breaths, phone calls, hours, meetings, destinations . . . Between saying hello and then good-bye again . . .

I could hear that the music had started. "Give me more red wine," I said. "I have to go."

chapter twenty-four

The Gershwin Room was crowded. I'd been in the front bar for hours, so the room was beginning to spin. It wasn't really how I'd imagined. I could hardly see the stage. The air was black and hot, and the carpet was sticky. I'd taken off my silver shoes. They were dangling from one hand, my wine was in the other. I was finding it hard to balance, but I kind of liked the darkness. You could be anyone in there. It was as if you could slip out of yourself, you could imagine yourself as better, deeper, more true. I could see parts of the stage; the sea of heads in front of me kept moving, so I kept moving too, from one tiptoe to the other, and in this boatlike way I caught glimpses of my Thin Captain. He was wearing a purple shirt with lilac vertical stripes. His hands were wrapped around the microphone and his feet were crossed, so that I kept thinking he might tip over. A big bit of hair fell in front of his eyes. Every now and then he jerked his head back to flick the hair away. I wondered why he didn't just push it back with his hand. He sung in this kind of jagged and jumpy way, like he had a pain, or an electrocution, but you could tell it was just the pain of rock and roll that he was channeling. Actually, I wasn't that convinced about the pain of rock and roll. In fact, I was most in love with him when he was just turning around and asking the guitar player a question. All that jerking and shouting and grunting made me feel like he was wanting to slam the sound of his voice right inside you, as if he didn't trust you to hear it otherwise. I admit I was prepared to forgive him anything, but generally I never like it when something yells at you for attention. I like seeing things that aren't asking to be looked at.

Once I saw a mynah bird land on my windowsill. It stared at the glass. It was an ugly teenage mynah bird with a fluffy head and bulbous hooded eyes. And even though I was only the distance of a small bush away from it, the young mutt couldn't even see me. I'd never been so close to a bird like that before; I could see the ridges on its yellow feet. After a while its mother flew in and dropped a worm in its gob and then flew away again. The mynah bird waited. The mother must have said, "Wait there, I've got some dessert coming." Anyway, I really loved watching it just standing there. It wasn't even beautiful or rare or balancing on one leg, it was just being itself. I thought of Harry Jacob and how when Harry played guitar, he just played it; he didn't try to get your attention with it. I wished the Thin Captain would act a bit more like a mynah bird. But I reasoned to myself that stars have the right to try to glitter as much as they can. You wouldn't catch a peacock dressed like a mynah bird.

In front of me there was a couple jostling. They were dancing, actually, only they weren't being very smooth about it. The boy was big, in a hulkish way, and he had a roaring warrior grin. She had spiky black hair and a tight lacy top, and she was round and squishy, and parts of her bulged out, like one of Ivy's pincushions. You could tell she liked being pushed around by that Viking boy. She didn't care about anything else, like whether she might be bumping into other people or looking foolish. Next to me there was a boy in a red T-shirt. He was holding a beer and he had nice brown arms. He wasn't talking to anyone either, but I didn't want to talk to him. I wanted to watch the Thin Captain. The jostling couple kept bumping into me and the boy in the red T-shirt. They were distracting me from my true mission, since I found myself watching them more than the stage, not because they looked good but because they were about the worst, bumpy, out-of-time dancers I'd ever seen and they weren't one bit embarrassed about it. I was fascinated by their lack of shame. My mother would have rolled her eyes if she could see them. Was I rolling my eyes? Not on the outside. I could tell that they were having a good time. Was I having a good time? They were all floppy with the fun they were having. I was standing stiff like a rusty anchor lodged in a forgotten place. So, I took a few liberties. I loosened my head from my neck. I let it float and lift. I softened down, sank into my body, away from other people's opinions. My eyes closed and opened. I was swaying and my arms were moving too. I was surrounded by music, I was buoyant and flowed like a weed in the ocean. I rippled, expanded, gave in to my beating heart and bones. I danced. The red T-shirt boy must have noticed I was behaving like a fun person, because he said something to me.

"What?" I said, because the music was loud.

"Like your dress," he repeated, leaning his mouth toward my ear. I turned and looked at him. He was dancing. I was dancing. We were dancing next to each other. If I added this up with the compliment he'd just leaned close to give me, I thought it might mean we were dancing together. I hoped this wasn't the case.

"Do you?" I said, rather stupidly.

"Yeah."

"Thanks." I turned my face to the floor because I was feeling awkward. I noticed my feet were bare. My shoes had once been in my hand but now they weren't. I frowned at my naked feet as if they'd misbehaved, but of course it wasn't their fault. It was the red wine that had set my mind adrift in a rather nice way. I'd been drunk a couple of times before. The first time was when Lucy and I went to Adam Allcot's New Year's Eve party. Lucy said I couldn't go in jeans, so she gave me a white dress that was short and had tiny red dots on it. Lucy didn't ever wear it because her legs weren't good, she said. It made my legs look brown, so I didn't mind. When we got there they gave us a glass of champagne. Adam Allcot's dad had a lot of money. There was a swimming pool with banana lounges around it. I remember those banana lounges especially because I was sitting on one when the champagne first hit me. I remember looking over at Lucy to see if she was feeling like I was. The only other thing I remember was that there was this older boy from school who pulled me into the garden and kissed me, and I didn't like it at all because his tongue went 'round and 'round in my mouth in a repulsive, urgent way, like he was having a race and not a kiss. And when I tried to get away he pushed me over on the grass and I got a grass mark on Lucy's white dress and I felt anxious in case it stained. After that the night was spoiled, because I wanted to go home and wash the dress before it was too late.

The red T-shirt boy wasn't that bad. He had talked to me, just like that, as if I was a regular nice girl who wouldn't think mean things. Maybe it wouldn't be so bad to dance with him. Maybe my dancing fun would be enhanced. The problem was that I didn't want to get stuck with him. Just say we started dancing and it wasn't fun. Then how would I stop? I didn't look at him, I looked straight ahead and tried to decide whether I should or shouldn't look.

"Can I get you a drink?" he said.

It was nice of him to ask, and I did even look again at his brown arms and think that they were the kind of arms I would like to have around me, but still, I didn't want him to get me a drink just in case it meant I owed him something. So I said, "No thanks," and he walked off. I knew he wouldn't come back. I started to feel almost lonely and regretful. I felt we'd been watching the band together, in an unspoken way, of course, and now I was left watching it alone. I wondered why I was so unfriendly; you'd think I preferred my own company, but I truly didn't. Maybe I was a cactus in my past life. Maybe I was a walrus.

Anyway, it felt as if that touch of regret and those six or eight glasses of red wine weren't mixing so well in my head, and then when I let the music in too, it all felt worse and much too much. I was slowly getting anxious and jammed in. I tried looking at the Thin Captain, but he wasn't looking at me. He was looking at the crowd. You could tell he loved the crowd, the thousand nameless faces merged into one. What he loved was the size of it. The dark swaying animal. I was in it. I was its eyes. He loved the eyes upon him. He was sucking in the love. My mind was falling around, spinning.

I threaded my way out.

Had the love been sucked out of me?

Did walruses ever feel lonely? Did they have brothers?

I sank onto the steps outside. To the passersby I would have looked like a wet old flag thrown over the step. The white concrete was cold and firm on my back. I liked the feel of it.

"You all right, lass?" said the bouncer, who looked like he should be doing a war dance but instead was just folding his large dark arms across his chest. I considered my beautiful dress, which was now unmistakably shabby because of the beer smear down the side. I considered my head, which felt not unlike my dress, sticky and wet with alcohol. I breathed in the ocean, and without trying to get up I said, "All things considered, yes, I'm all right."

"Well, you can't lie there, someone's likely to step on you." He had a tattoo of an anchor on his forearm. Maybe, I wondered in a seesaw way, it was a sign, or maybe it wasn't. But I didn't want to move. Not one bit. So I groaned and hoped it might make him a bit more sympathetic to my situation.

"You had too much to drink, lass?"

"Yes," I said, a bit curtly I suspect, because his sympathy seemed to wane suddenly.

"Look, if you're gonna have a chuck, there's toilets out the back. I'm afraid I'll have to ask you to get up now." He stood right over me, like a shadow. I groped around and stood up, leaning on the banister, glaring at him feebly. I hated anyone telling me what to do.

The thought of going back in there made me feel weary. But I couldn't give up. I didn't want to be in that room, but I had to go back for him, the Thin Captain. I swelled up with air. I was ready. I was swaying and breathing and charged with love. I plunged back in.

chapter twenty-five

Luckily, the music had finished and people were dispersing or assembling around the bar. There was no one onstage. The Thin Captain had disappeared. I would find him, though. He had asked me to come. He would want me to find him. He would be expecting me. He would say, "Ah, here is the girl in the red dress. I'm so glad you came." He would —

"You got a pass, lady?" I'd found the backstage door.

"What pass?"

"A backstage pass. Can't let you in without a pass, sorry."

"But I was invited."

"Sorry, lady. You need a pass." He crossed his arms and acted like a brick wall. I was standing there, brimming with despair, when another man put his arm around my shoulders.

"It's okay, Ron, she's with me," he said to the brick-wall man. It was like magic: The man automatically stepped aside, and in we walked. Just like that. I felt the way Moses must have felt when the

Red Sea parted. The man with the magic was almost bald, but he wasn't old, just bald. He was sweaty too, and his skin was white, but there was a blue tinge about him. He had eyes like a cat and, though he kept his arm around my shoulders and took me into the room, I wasn't sure he was real.

It all seemed to happen in an instant. I didn't have time to thank him, or inquire, before — there I was, in the band room, the out-of-bounds room for only the most special people.

It was a small, ugly room. There was a couch against one wall, a table in the middle with cut-up fruit and cheese on it, a line of mirrors, and a fridge. There were people, groups of them, smoking and talking and laughing. They seemed older than me. I saw the Thin Captain straightaway. He didn't see me. He was talking to a girl on the couch. His arm was around her.

"So, who invited you?" said the bald man. I saw the groups of people looking at me. I stood out. The red dress. It was wrong. It was dramatic and loud. I wanted to turn it down. I wanted to blend in. I stared wildly at the bald man. I couldn't speak. I couldn't say who invited me. Some spurt of laughter snaked up out of a corner in the room and I could feel my thoughts stand up like hackles. It was as if, up till now, those poor sun-sodden thoughts had been plodding around like fat lazy queens in long cloaks and, upon entering the band room, had suddenly started to run fast and get very thin and alarmed. I tried not to pay any attention to them. I tried for an instant to fix my mind on a simple thing, like the wet shine on the bald head in front of me, but before I could stop it, those runaway thoughts were having me thinking I was surrounded entirely by crocodiles. Large, laughing, upstanding crocodilish people wearing snappish expressions. It wasn't that the people had uncommonly large jaws or threatening teeth, it was just that the air around me seemed ferocious.

I heard a conversation going on about haircuts. Someone was pointing out someone else's bald patch. Then there was a white-haired girl in tight pants who was talking about skydiving and getting engaged to the bald patch, all on the same day. How thrilling, I thought to myself, mainly to test out my ability to make a normal observation. The engaged girl was bending over to butt her cigarette, and I saw she was wearing those underpants that only have a strap up the back. You could see them poking up from her tight pants. It started me thinking about my silver shoes, which led naturally to the realization that I wasn't wearing them right when I most needed to be making an impression. Worst of all, I was standing barefoot in the middle of a band room, with a back-pack containing a book of ocean paintings and a head containing crocodiles.

"Oh, you're a fan!" smirked the bald man in response to my speechlessness. "You wanna speak to Frank?" He jerked his chin in the Thin Captain's direction.

"No." I breathed the word out, desperate to make him stay next to me. I realized that a fan was the lowliest of the low and though technically I really wasn't a fan, I certainly didn't want to be thrust over there. At least not until the thought aerobics had settled. I tried to tell myself that there was no reason for me to feel crocodiled; after all, they were just people like me, only a bit older and with sexier underpants and musical instruments. The bald man frowned. He wasn't a philosopher. In fact, none of them were talking about human suffering or foreign policy. They weren't discovering antibodies or saving forests or even painting pictures that make your heart leap, so why should I feel so squashed down and eaten up by them?

"I'm the drummer. Did you see the gig or what?"

"Mmm. I saw. But not much. Too crowded." He nodded and walked over to the fridge.

"Wanna beer?"

"Yeah, thanks." I didn't want one. I hated beer. But I wanted to keep him with me. I wanted him to shelter me. I didn't care who he was or what he said, as long as he would stand next to me. He was a shape I could hide behind, blend into. At least, with him, I was part of a people clump. I was feeling so jellyfish, so soft and internal and small.

It's no use hiding behind him. They all think you're an idiot, said Mean Person. They know you're a faker. I argued feebly that maybe they were like Pedigree Disco Girl: nice on the inside. Maybe they didn't even notice me. But I couldn't convince myself.

The bald guy gave me a beer and I leaned up on the bench, just to give a casual waiting air, but I knew it was affected and I couldn't get it right. So I sighed and stopped trying. I said to myself bravely, "Oh, who cares what they think?" And though Mean Person snorted dubiously, I took a swig of beer and, as proof of my defiance, stole another look at the Thin Captain.

He was fiddling with a champagne glass which had a broken stem, balancing it on his thigh. He wasn't talking to the girl. The guy who had the recently lamented bald patch was sitting on the edge of the couch, and the Thin Captain was laughing with him. But the girl sat on the other side of them, and I died a little inside to see his arm flung around her. It definitely was. I'd hoped I'd seen it wrong the first time, but the arm was there. She didn't appear nervous either. She had her legs crossed and she was smiling. She had a pretty face, hair rusty like autumn leaves, pale skin, green shirt, jeans, and sandals. She was gazing around the room as if looking for something a little more interesting than the haircut conversation. She saw me looking at her, but if she thought anything you couldn't tell. She leaned on the Thin Captain and said she was tired. He patted her leg and kept talking to the bald patch. She closed her eyes momentarily and sank back into the couch with a big sigh. He turned to her and said she could always get a cab if she wanted to leave. She nodded vaguely and reached for a glass of wine, as if she didn't care, as if she wasn't going to make trouble. You could tell he didn't like to be bothered.

I turned my back to them. I was vaguely aware that the drummer was speaking to me but I'd not heard a word. Why was I so dressed up? That's what the drummer wanted to know. I don't know, I was saying, wanting to get out. My mind was racing. I felt as if I was caving in, as if any minute I might just shrivel up and everyone would point in horror. "Look! Silly girl has shriveled up."

"Frankie, you going?" the drummer was speaking now to him, the Thin Captain. I felt weak. They were coming toward us. Thin Captain and the girl. Both of them. I didn't look. I looked down. "Not coming out?" persisted the drummer.

"Nuh, we're going home," said the Thin Captain. He was next to me. I could see her, the bottom half of her anyway. She wasn't holding his hand.

"See ya then," said the drummer, lightly, as if it didn't matter.

"Yeah, have a good one," said the Thin Captain, and as he said it he tossed a glance at me. He looked down at me as if I was a speck of dirt on his shoe. Not even his shoe, the drummer's shoe. I was something for the drummer to kick off. He didn't even recognize me. Everyone in there must have seen that I was just a fan who didn't even get a mere hello.

"Bye, Lana," said the drummer.

"Bye," said the girl. She gave me an uncertain smile. I knew she felt sorry for me. And somehow I felt sorry for her too. I don't know why, but suddenly she seemed so very sad to me. It even occurred to me that if she'd been at my school, she and I could have been friends.

chapter twenty-six

By the time I got out of there it was late and the streets were emptying, which was lucky because I was feeling private. If I could have, I would have yanked the self out of my body and put it in the bin or covered it with dirt. I sat for a while on a low brick wall, pulled my knees up, and put my head on them. I saw myself spilling all over the street, pouring into the pavement like melted ice cream, people having to step over me on their way to the beach in the morning. What a mess I would make on the street. People like Mrs. Mrs. Porrit would say, "Did you see Manon Clarkeson? Late in the night she poured herself all over the street. Just like her to make a mess. She always was a hopeless child."

And my mother would be ashamed. She wouldn't talk about it, though, not to anybody. My dad would hurry over and clean up the mess.

Once, I tried to make a birthday cake for Dad, as a surprise. I admit I got a bit creative with it: I didn't follow the recipe exactly, and it came out looking like a badly shaped hat. But I put candles on it anyway, and when I took it to the table Mum poked it with a fork and laughed. She said, "Oh, why are you so hopeless, Manon?" I didn't answer her, since I didn't know why I was so hopeless, but Eddie took a piece. It looked pretty messy on his plate. He said it tasted fine, but Mum snorted. Dad didn't say a word. After that I never made another cake. I'm just not the baking type. But I could still hear people snorting at me. Mean Person was a champion snorter. Mean Person, of course, had a few snort-infected words to say. Oh, boy, first you make a complete dickhead of yourself, and now you're getting maudlin. What did I tell you? You're hopeless.

I was sick of that word *hopeless*. It had been dumped on me a long time ago, as if it was a dunce hat, as if I would always be somewhat incapable, unable to steer myself properly through life, unable to put out a fire, to roast a chicken, or wear a nice dress. It was like having a curse put on you. You can't help but believe it, because you always believe what they tell you. And before you even know it, you've become a hopeless mean old word-dumper yourself.

It was like when you saw a mean snarling dog and you thought to yourself, "I mustn't be scared because the dog will sense my fear and attack me." But that very thought, that the dog will sense your fear, is such a scary thought that you get another fear: the fear of being found out fearing. Life seemed to be full of those snarling dogs, making you dislike your own disliking, making you afraid of your own fears, making you try too hard to cover them up, making you put a red dress over your own thin lost limbs. Who was I convincing? I looked at the sky, all lit up with stars. A couple walked past me. They slanted forward as they walked, her with her hairdo and him with his sheltering arm. You could tell they were in agreement, by the way they strode. It was as if the ideas that dwelled within them, and sought a future place, had risen up and joined in a blaze of joyous certainty, so that the couple only had to keep pushing forward through the black warm air toward that one clear star. Their star. "Their star," I said again in my mind, and then I wished I hadn't said it.

I had my hunger wires all mixed up. It was as if I had this large, large hole in my heart and I was trying to plug it up with a thin, thin man. Any kid old enough to do a jigsaw puzzle would tell you that a thin bit won't fill a large hole. So why was I such a dope?

See, it wasn't the Thin Captain curling me in, it wasn't him, the handsome, slightly successful person; it was the feeling of him not liking me. It was the way I agreed so wholeheartedly with him not liking me that I didn't like me either. So now there were two people not liking me. Him and me. Of course, I was the more important disliker in the equation, since I knew myself better and my opinion counted for more, but still, having all that disliking jabbing into you can really knock you out; it can make you feel very bad and very unlikable.

"Their star," I said again and remembered the night when Harry first kissed me. Just before, when we were looking up at the stars, he said that we weren't really seeing the stars, we were seeing the light they cast and it wasn't a direct light, it was a sideways light. Whatever it was I wanted, it wasn't a direct, exact thing; it wasn't the star, it wasn't the thing at all, it was the light that came off things. Maybe it was the dark too. Maybe it was the thing that makes you pulse and dance and run deep in the woods, like a wild animal. It was the mist of those paintings. . . .

And that kind of stuff can't be named or explained with a voice. It's a knowing that becomes your blood before you even know your heart has opened. It comes in sideways, slips through your pores while you're busy trying something else. It slips in while you're failing at badminton, injuring your arm, standing alone. It whispers so softly it isn't you who hears it, it's yourself, or your soul, or whatever it is that dwells within.

I knew I had one of those: a drawn-in, torn-up, tossed-to-the-sky self. A self that made a slow silent passage. A self that longed to become me, like a breath becomes sky. What I wanted was to join up with the world, to become one piece of blue.

I said to myself, "You just fell over and now you have to get up and keep going."

No one likes that falling over. But then hardly anyone likes exercise or cabbage either, and they're still supposed to be good for you. I can't say I was completely convinced by this startling, cabbage-flavored blast of good sense, and I could even feel my sorry old mind, with its hearty appetite for high drama, revolting at the very whiff of it. But I just heaved a big sigh and decided there was only one thing to do, and that was move.

I got up off the wall. My bare feet felt the footpath and I looked at them poking out from my dress like little white mice. I felt fond of them. I don't know why. Probably because they'd always been there, whenever I expected them to be, and I knew they would walk me away.

holding your head up

chapter twenty-seven

It must have been about two o'clock in the morning by the time I'd made my way up Tennyson Street. There was no one about. My bike was still locked up at the beach, but I had my backpack and my book of nocturnes. I wasn't thinking. I was just going. Tennyson Street was a long street lined with an arch of spreading plane trees. There were lovely, dark, soft houses, old curving apartments, muffled gardens, curtained windows, upstairs rooms. People sleeping inside them. Families without holes. With warm safe houses. No silent places. I kept looking at the homes. Walking and looking.

Number 3/37. Would it be a lovely warm home too? As I came close, I had the strange feeling that I had been there before, as if the street had once flowed briefly through my memory. But I was always having these feelings, because I always dreamed of other places, imagined myself in boats, in velvet, on sweeping lawns under huge spreading trees, in a calm stone house with wide windows. Number 37 was a block of flats. Brick flats with a thin cement driveway and a gaping carport at the end. A big yellow globe stuck out on the wall, lighting up the bulging steel balconies. One had flowerpots and plastic furniture. The others were empty, except for an air-conditioning unit. I felt vaguely anxious as I stood in the driveway, not because the flats looked sinister, more because I'd known something once and I'd forgotten it.

I walked up a stairwell. Number 3 was exactly the same as number 1 and number 2. It's so much easier to be the same, I thought. At least number 3 had the sound of a television coming from inside, but no lights were on. I pulled back the knocker and held it still for an instant. Suddenly I was only a tiny, tiny distance away from finding out who Eddie knew here, and instead of feeling excited I felt like a dying fish in a bucket. If there was one thing I was getting sure of lately, it was that if you expect something to make a difference it surely won't. I was stupid for counting on it, I was stupid for even coming. I tried looking at it sideways but it didn't work. All I saw was that little hole in the door that people look through to see you standing there as if you are a small bulging person in a pond. There was no largeness coming out that door. I was looking for Wise Person. I was imagining that she would explain something. A thing I didn't know, a thing that would help me not be so mad.

You see, I hadn't forgiven Eddie, not yet. I hadn't forgiven him for leaving me here alone. Well, it wasn't Eddie I was mad at, it was life. I was all rare in my heart about it, if you know what I mean, it felt all bloodied and soft and undercooked in there. Ever since it had happened, the days had rolled over, one after the other like breathing, unmanaged, just arriving and then leaving. There was nothing to mark one day out from the other. It was like a road without signposts or corners; it wore at my edges, the even tumble of day after day, each darkened by a wedge of night. I was waiting for something, anything: thunder, a truth, a new heart. I began to hope that it would be different, that a corner would be turned, a day would open its red mouth and cry out for wine. And right now, I had imagined, would be the moment that would open its red mouth. So why was I feeling so unsure of everything?

I told myself I didn't really want that, as if God was listening, because he never gave me what I wanted. You can't fool God, though, just like you can't pretend to a snarling dog that you aren't scared.

And even if Wise Person was behind that door, would she want to see me? I convinced myself that it didn't matter what she might think, since I'd come all this way. Surely I was sick of caring about what other people thought, and wasn't it about time I left some room for me to think my own thoughts and not other people's thoughts. I flapped the knocker into the door. Three times. It felt good to get it over and done with.

At first there was no response. I pressed my ear to the door. I thought I could hear shuffling or sniffing or something, but then it was quiet. I knocked again. This time there was a firm response. More moving and then feet coming toward the door. At the door the feet stopped. Whoever was on the other side was looking at me through that hole. I could feel their eyes sharpening through it. I stared at my bare feet. I didn't let myself imagine what I would look like to those eyes, but I couldn't look straight back at that little hole.

Whoever D. Wolton was, she seemed to be considering. Did she recognize me? I thought suddenly of Eddie's eyes. The way they hurried over the world, scouring it, not stopping, like a crow flying low against the paddocks. And me, waiting, with a big mess in my heart.

A long sniff came from behind the door. Then it began to open.

chapter twenty-eight

I recognized D. Wolton immediately and I felt sick. It wasn't Demeter, or Delia either. He leaned on the door. His underarm faced me, his face leering behind it like Luna Park. Travis Houghton.

"Little Manon," he said. I stared back at him. "Well, what in the hell are you doing, knocking on my door at this time? You realize what time it is? It's two o'bloody clock!"

"I didn't know it was you."

"Yeah? Well, you do now." He sniffed again. He was bare, apart from a pair of pajama pants. One hand was hooked over the top of his pants. I remembered then. How Dad and I were in the car, in that driveway. How Mum had rushed out of the stairwell, clutching a dressing gown around her. How Dad had said it and how she'd sunk onto that cement driveway, those balconies looking down over her, when she sobbed and shook like a two-year-old. Dad had got out of the car and helped her up.

"You looking for somewhere to stay, are you?" Travis yawned.

"No." I just stood there. I had nothing left now. I felt a big gust of hope rush out of me and I was emptied, hollow as an old exploded balloon. He shrugged and folded his arms across his chest.

"Well, whaddya want then? You look like a hooker, you know that? You look like a bloody hooker. You're lucky no one picked you up."

I started to cry. I swiped at the tears, but he saw.

"For God's sake! Don't start that on me. You better come in." He walked away from the door. All I knew was that I wanted to go home, but my legs walked me in because my legs weren't thinking.

There was a small room with a big television and stereo in the corner. There were two matching brown couches and a table in the middle with an ashtray, a bong, and a neat pile of *Rolling Stone* magazines. Frothy nylon curtains that made you think of old-lady underpants covered the window. They were meant to be white, but they were gray and motionless. A fan stood in one corner, next to a big shelf full of records. The room smelled of incense. I sat down on the couch that faced the window. Travis sprawled on the other couch. I found myself staring at a ceramic breast that was sitting on top of a speaker. It was hollow, with a hole in the nipple where you could pour through.

"It's a jug," said Travis, grinning. I quickly turned away from it. "You get it? A jug." He let out a short stab of laughter. I felt embarrassed, as if it were my breast he was laughing at. So I just stared at the carpet. I guess I'd lost my sense of humor.

"Tell you what you need," he said. "A choof."

"What's that?"

"You know, a billy. Does a world of good when you're down." He leaned toward the little table and tapped at the bong. "I'll pack you a cone if you like." I nodded feebly. I didn't care that much anymore; not about the Thin Captain, not about Paris. I felt like getting quiet. I felt like getting really quiet.

Travis set to work, grinding and stuffing and fussing around looking for a lighter.

"So, I hear your mum went back to France to live."

"Mmm," I said. "She's with her family there. Her sister." I narrowed my eyes at Travis. I didn't want him talking about her, actually, as if he had some kind of claim. I remembered what Ivy had told me.

"Mum lied to everyone, Travis. To you as well." I don't know what made me say it. Maybe I wanted to twist up Travis's reality too.

"Whaddya mean, Manon? What are you saying?"

"She was never an actress. She lied. She came out with that theater company, but she was only the costume hand. You know, she didn't even come from Paris either. She came from a place called Poitiers. She was just a seamstress." I said this last sentence in a bitter old drunken way and I even added a snort. Travis didn't seem to care one bit. He just roared with laughter. "That'd be right," he said, and started packing the cone, shaking his head in an amused way.

Ivy said Dad didn't care either. He had written to Mum's sister, because he was so worried about Mum with her depression. The sister wrote back and told him the truth about Mum. The sister said their mother was an alcoholic who died when they were young. Mum had some liaison with a married man and ended up pregnant. She had an abortion, and that was when her depression started.

Dad never even told Mum he knew. He didn't care that she'd lied to him, didn't care that she wasn't an actress. None of that mattered, he didn't give a hoot what she'd done, he just loved her. He loved her so much that he just let her go on telling her stories about being an actress. He even organized little parties so she could have the pleasure of telling, of being the center of attention. Mum wanted everyone to think she was special, and she was safe here. She could pretend whatever she wanted, and there was no one to contradict it. Ivy said Mum had even somehow convinced herself, the way she carried on.

It was the one fine thing about Mum: She was an actress. The one thing I was proud of, the one thing that made up for her unusual behavior. Ivy said she would have made a great actress, anyway. But that didn't count.

Travis passed me the bong. It was made of an old Spring Valley bottle and a piece of plastic pipe with a coat hanger wound around the bottom to make it stand up. I'd never had one before but I'd seen Eddie doing it, so I didn't tell Travis I was a beginner. It must have been obvious, because he interrupted me when I started to try and light up.

"No, no, you've got to hold the shoddy, here, look, with your thumb." He grabbed it to show me how. I wasn't even sure I wanted it. Boy, it ponged. I should have known it was bad, just by the way it stunk. I mean, if you offered that to a hungry horse to eat, would they even go near it? I doubt it. Horses have fine instincts. As for mine, they'd been blunted by alcohol and disappointment. One after the other.

It made a dirty gurgle as I breathed in the smoke, which seemed to shoot straight up into my brain. I felt sick and dizzy all at once. My head started to turn. I sank back into the couch as Travis laughed.

"Head spins, huh?" I nodded and closed my eyes for a minute. My head seemed to waft away. I felt lighter.

"Travis?" I said, when I'd recovered a bit.

"Yep." He was packing himself one. I was pinned down to the couch. My head was light but my body was filled with heaviness. I was glad I'd got heavy enough to slow down.

"Why do you reckon Eddie would've written down your address?"

Travis stopped for an instant and frowned, then he began nodding to himself.

"Ah, so that's how come you got here." He chuckled. He put his mouth to the bong and breathed in a long hard breath. He held the smoke down in his lungs for as long as he could, then he blew it out, one long stinky ribbon of smoke.

"Probably because Eddie was coming here, the night he was — the night of the accident. He was on his way here. Didn't you know that?" I tried to sit up but it made me feel nauseous, so I sank back into the couch.

"No, they were going to see a band. Harry wanted to see a band," I said. Travis raised his eyebrows.

"Is that what Harry said?"

"Yeah. That's what he said."

Travis flopped back into his couch.

"Well, then, Harry was covering. For your mother."

"What d'you mean?"

"Look, I heard your mother ring Eddie. She was hysterical. Wasn't my fault. Don't mean to be rude, but she was a damn moody bitch, your mother. Almost the moment we got here she started complaining. After a couple of weeks she was always bawling her bloody eyes out. She'd ring your brother, telling him I was abusing her. Wasn't true. Never laid a hand on her. But Eddie was coming to get her. I heard her give him the address. She went and packed her bag and she waited all night for him. Right there. Right where you are now. Perched on the couch like a little owl. You look like her, you know? Did you know that? Only you're younger, of course."

I didn't answer him, so he kept on. "Anyway, she wouldn't speak to me. But I was glad she was going. She should never have come. If you ask me, she had a bloody screw loose."

I wasn't listening to Travis, though. I was thinking back to the last time I saw Eddie. We were on my bed, talking about Harry. The phone was ringing and Eddie jumped up to get it. He went out of my room and then, that was it. He went to answer the phone. He never came back.

"When did she ring? I mean, what time?" I was weak.

"Dunno what time. It was evening time."

"What about Harry? Why was he in the car?" My voice was slurring.

"Probably just being a mate, I reckon. Helping out."

"Mmm." I could hardly get a word out. I saw words forming in my mind, like little insects clinging to a piece of fruit. A great ripe soft piece of fruit. I heard myself take a deep breath. Minutes must have gone by in that one long breath. My eyelids were heavy, I couldn't keep them apart.

"You can sleep there if you want. On the couch. I've got a blanket," said Travis.

"Okay," I heard myself mumble. The smoke was in my bruised mind, going in loops like a little kid's handwriting. The wine. My mum. She's bitten by the wind again. A screw loose. She never told us she'd called Eddie. She let Harry cover it up. Harry Jacob. She's bitten by the wind again. Bitten by Travis Houghton. Travis was looking at me. Travis leering. Travis getting up.

He gave me a blanket and left the room.

chapter twenty-nine

I dreamed that Eddie and I were in a queue. We were going somewhere. The men at a desk let Eddie through because he had the right ticket, but I didn't. I was looking in my bag, for another type of ticket or a passport or something, and Eddie was walking beyond the double doors. He was going on a boat. I was annoyed. I wanted to go too, but the men wouldn't let me go.

I don't know how long I slept. Maybe it was only an hour or so. And it wasn't that I woke up; something woke me. Just like that night when I'd sensed my dad sitting on my bed. Only this time it wasn't my dad.

It was still dark, but I could make out the bulk of Travis hovering over me. I couldn't see his face, only the blackened looming shape of him. The floor groaned under the weight of his body.

"What?" I said. He hadn't spoken, but I didn't like the quiet coming out of him. I wanted him to speak so that he would stop being that dark breathing bulk, that readiness. Surely, once there were words, normal little words and explanations, out in the air, *pop*, like that, then the tight deadly quiet would be broken and the lights would go on and all the dark shapes in the room would again become couches and lamps and ceramic breasts and normal things.

He put his hand on my leg but he didn't speak.

"Travis?" I said sharply. I started to sit up, to wake us both up properly and sort it out. Maybe he was sleepwalking. He bent down toward me. I don't know what happened next — if his hands came toward me, or if my body jumped up. The hands went like claws to my shoulder. His knee jammed over my thighs. I felt a rush of horror, real horror. I knew what was happening. It was night and Travis was on top of me. He was trying to get sexy. His breath smelled bad. I turned away.

"What the hell are you doing, Travis?" I knew exactly what he was doing, but I wanted to give him a chance to get out of it nicely, pretend he had made a mistake. His mouth was on my neck, a wet wormy tongue. I squirmed away. He didn't say, "Beg your pardon, Manon, I just fell." He said, "It's all right, Manon. I won't hurt you. It'll be nice. You're gonna like it. Come on, relax."

His voice was whispery, sugary, like I'd never heard it. It wasn't the usual Travis. I thought of Pervert Man. I thought of Ruth Warlock. I knew he wasn't going to be nice about this.

"Get off me, Travis." This time I didn't even try to say it nicely. His body pressed down on top of mine; it didn't just lie there, it pushed downward, as if he was trying to grind my bones. I was jammed underneath. His hands were moving fast and he was pulling at my red dress. I didn't want my red dress pulled down like that. I was pulling it back on and he was pulling it off. It was stupid. I was feeling mad since it was my dress and my body but he was acting like it was his. I yelled at him to get off but he just kept saying, "Shhh shhhh, you'll like it, you'll like it." I wasn't liking it one bit. I was hating it. His hands felt bad. I couldn't stop them; they searched under my dress as if I'd stolen a million dollars and was hiding it under there.

So I can't be blamed for what happened next. It wasn't so much me who did it, it was my hand. My hand getting back at Travis's hands. My left hand, to be precise. It reached out toward the table, fumbled with the empty bottles, grabbed a large one, and then I watched the hand bring the bottle down on Travis's head, as hard as it could. Harder than I could've done it, were it me and not my hand. I heard it connect: a dull wet thud and a shattering. For a tiny second everything stopped. I was shocked at what my hand had done. Had I killed him?

I didn't have time for this concern to take hold of me before his head jerked up and he screamed. He rolled to his side, moaning. I wasn't stopping to listen. Once I knew he wasn't dead, I was pulling my dress up, scrambling off the couch, quick as I could. My heart was thumping in my chest as if it were trying to get out itself.

"Bitch," he yelled. "You little bitch." I fumbled in the dark for my backpack and yelled out, "Sorry." I wasn't one bit sorry. It was just my habit to apologize, especially as I'd just injured a man twice my size. Fear can make you tell lies. Besides, there was no way I was leaving my book of nocturnes with Travis. I was finding them and I was getting out. I saw that I'd broken the bong on his head. There was a very bad smell. He was trying to stand up, staggering, with his hand across the back of his head. He was yelling really foul words at me, which I don't care to repeat. I grabbed my pack and I ran down the stairwell and I ran down the dark street, past the lovely, safe houses. I didn't stop running till I was almost at the beach again.

chapter thirty

I headed for the beach the way a heart heads for home, running all the way there and then stopping still and staring out, breath thudding away over the black spreading sea. Not a single other person was there. Just the thin torn waves scratching at the shore, and a couple of seagulls wheeling around the dark sky, their bodies eerie, silent and pink in the glow from the city. Fuzzy dots of light shone out from the factories around the bay, like the long-distance eyes of a stranger, blinking back at you, uncomprehending.

If you keep running and running in one direction, sooner or later you come to the end of land and face the sea, and then you have to stop. You have to consider. The sea asks that of you.

But the thought of considering made me panic and I looked for my bike instead, since it was something I belonged to. It was still leaning against the No Standing pole, looking strangled and abandoned, so I didn't look at it for long. Still puffing, I flopped down on the cold gray sand. I grabbed handfuls and poured it on my ankles, as if I was digging myself in, as if I was another beach fixture, like the rubbish bin with its hat of hot chip packets and empty cans.

Mean Person was edging to get a word in. I knew I had to stop this happening; if I let Mean Person start on about me being the only person in the whole world who was awake and alone and with nowhere to go and a bad-man experience burning inside and not even a pair of shoes let alone a hand to hold, then that would be the end of me. I had to make a friend pretty quickly or I might just die of aloneness right then and there. Can you die of that? I had a mouse that did. It was called Dora and it died after Flora ran away. It stopped running around in its wheel. I found its little stiff body lying dead still in the wheel.

What a tiny frail heart a mouse must have.

I could hear the soft, fat ebbing of the ocean's body against the beach, like it had a heartbeat itself. An on-and-on, never-ending heartbeat. Small sounds of birdsong threaded through the air, and the stars were fading like an old smattering of dust. I felt like a spy, witnessing the quiet private time when night slipped into dawn. As if it was undressing.

I made out to myself that the tall lights, with their showers of yellow air falling on the sand, were great upstanding wise figures like Abraham Lincoln and Nelson Mandela and Mr. Jesus Christ himself. Also Mr. Higgie from the Castlemaine chemist, who is always kind and wears a safe white coat. And I couldn't leave out Mr.

Whistler, who painted those paintings in my bag, because I knew for sure that, whoever he was, he would understand.

Or would he?

If he came along right now and saw me, he'd think I was like a broken-down car that had driven too fast over too many bumps. He'd think I'd lost my wings. He'd think I was a fudged-up kids' kite.

I'd always figured that those despairing wings had lost their body, but maybe it was the body that had lost its wings? Or maybe it didn't matter what gets lost, maybe it's just once you've lost something you always expect that someone will come along and fix you up again. You're waiting for it. So there's another type of waiting. You're waiting for someone to know you're not really a fudged-up kids' kite, you're just a person whose heart's got a hole or two, or you're just a pair of wings whose body fell away. I knew then why I'd felt bad about leaving those wings hanging there. I was the one who knew them, knew how they really were. It was my job to know that they were really a glorious bird, waiting to be fixed, to be whole again. Who would know it now that I'd gone?

I was looking at the ocean and it was looking back at me, combing the shore with its little white-edged waves, like fingers stroking you, like how Ivy stroked my back, soft and on and on, like pulling out knots . . . enough to make you give in. I sighed, not for me but for the ocean. What a job, being the ocean, being the weeping of the world, offering with its body, a lament: an endless underlying call of again and again. Wave after wave. Again and again. There's a pattern to all this, I thought.

It was me who had to know I was all right. I couldn't keep waiting for someone else to know it, because no one else could. Only that small blade of self, leaning in the wind.

I did a very important thing right then. I stood up. It may seem like a simple motion, but believe me it was a great glorious victory. It was as if I was reversing the wind, shaking the stillness out of a rock, draining the despair out of a drooping wing. I didn't feel like standing, I felt like lying down and curling up on my side like a leaf that knows it's heading for a drain. But I thought of Dora the mouse, I thought of those wings, and I lifted my arms up and made myself as big as I could. I kept thinking to myself, "Boy, I'm good at being big. Look at me, I'm huge, I'm swooping, I'm carousing, I'm Hollywood. Look at me, I'm moving."

I started to swoop along the beach, running at the water's edge.

Unfortunately, Travis's hands came rudely back into my mind and to stop them I had to think of Harry's hands. Harry's lovely hands, never expecting anything from anyone. I only intended to remember the look of them. I always did admire the look of his hands. They were wide. They were men's hands but they held life so softly. They were new and gentle and I couldn't help remembering how they touched, even though I was not intending to remember that. The night, by the Springs, I felt Harry's hands going under my clothes, and I could tell those hands knew about love. I felt my body under his hands, like I'd never felt it before. I felt it getting warm and hungry. And when we opened our eyes, his hand was on my leg and he said, "I like your leg." I smiled because it seemed to me that perhaps he knew my leg. I said, "Harry, let me confess, my leg likes you." And I watched his hands gently pulling at the buttons on my shirt.

The next day he took me to school on his brother's motorbike. When he leaned forward, I leaned into him and rested my head sideways on his back. I closed my eyes to feel the wind like a cave around me. We were going fast, carving out the face of day: sun spilled in the tunnel of trees, a splattered sky, shining, burnt colors of leaves, chunks of light gleaming in and out of shadow. I felt as if I'd been untied. When he pressed my leg, something in me leaned closer toward him. He was dark and anonymous in his helmet. He could've been a prince. He could've been a dangerous man.

I told Sharon Baker. (You have to tell someone. It's almost like doing it again, in the telling of it, even in the remembering.)

"I kissed Harry Jacob," I whispered.

"Wow," she breathed out. She was really much nicer than Lucy. She wasn't a know-all, and I'd long since worked out that eczema wasn't contagious. "Was he a good kisser? I bet he was."

"The best," I said, as if I'd kissed a million others.

"How far did you go? Did you do it?" she asked.

I didn't answer her right then. I just grinned. I was a new person. But that was my secret self.

I was walking, feet in the shallows. You couldn't tell, if you watched, whether the darkness was fading out of the sky or whether the light was seeping in. I knew that soon the sun would rise and people would come in their white jogging shoes, puffing up and down the beach. The trams would start rattling and clanking and cars would zoom past. The day would creak into action, just like any other day. And the night would be wiped away, snuffed out by the light and action and white sneakers jogging, as if there wasn't really madness and shame and regret; there was just this onwardness, the world heading forward.

It must have been about five o'clock in the morning. I took off my red dress, I lifted it over my head and let it drop on the sand where it lay like a dying puddle. I walked into the water, stepping over the small, charging waves. The cold swept through me, clear and ringing. I felt the morning air enclose me. I was happy to be cleaning everything off: Travis, the bong water, the band room, the extinguished hope, the red dress, especially that. . . . Boy, it felt good to be out of that dress. That dress was my mother's dress and not mine and even though she was in me, I was in me too. And I was the one wearing this self. It didn't have to be red. Blue, I thought, blue is the largest color.

I stood in the sea up to my waist, my fingers pulling through the water. The horizon stretched out like the world's first and last line. An untouchable line. An eternal, knowing kind of line. I knew there was an importance lying along the horizon and I half expected it to confess itself to me. I even listened for the sound of a collision. What an effort it must be to separate the sky from the sea.

It made you think. If the horizon is what distinguishes one thing from another, says this is this and this is that, then it is the horizon that gives you the feeling that there is an ending, a final place where one thing will meet another, a place to go toward.

But it wasn't really like that, because if you listened to it, you couldn't hear that final place, you could only hear the waves coming again and again, as if they were the horizon's own breath, nudging the sand into different slopes and ripples, leaving their ribbons of foam and winding heaps of bone and shell, all worn smooth by some insistent caress, some long journey, some distant tiny collision, over and over. You see the waves continue, sometimes small or sighing, or sweeping in fans, or pounding the shore like an angry fist, still just continuing. It makes you wonder if there isn't really somewhere to arrive at, if it isn't all just continuing, and continuing. It makes you suspect that there might not be any final discoveries that will turn the world back up the right way.

To wander without trying to find something. Imagine that. Imagine what might fall out of the air.

Once I found a paper nautilus shell, just like that, just as if it had fallen out of the air. I was walking, pushing myself forward through the ocean, at Lorne, waist-deep, one arm hovering above me, wrapped in a plaster cast. My broken arm was a new limb, jutting out white and dirty. The same one I had in Ivy's photo. The one I was proud of. I did forward rolls with it. And I went swimming. There was no reason to be looking for something, I was just seeing how I could move through the water without wetting the plaster. My foot felt it, just its edge, just a fine and tender frilled lip.

Not everyone gets to stumble onto something perfect. I put it on the mantelpiece at home, up with Eddie's footy trophies. It wasn't that it was beautiful and rare; it was the rare and beautiful fact of finding it. A vulnerable truth that had chosen me, edged itself impossibly out of the sand, whole and white. Proof that life will find you best when you aren't looking for it. When you aren't trying to work it out.

I stretched out my arms and stroked the top of the sea with my palms. And since I was feeling emotional, I let my arms spin 'round and 'round, driving them through the water. Then I sank down into it. I went right under and swam along the line of the shore, reaching with my arms. It was a long time since I'd swum in the sea. A summer holiday, years and years ago.

Those memories belonged to a land that was always behind me. A land of shadows, untouchable, unchanging, and completely mine.

A scent could take me there. The smell of the sea and there I was swimming at Lorne, Eddie, always swimming out deeper, diving under, calling out "Hey, Clapot! Watch this!"

I lay on my back in the sea and looked up. The sky pressed against me. I let it lay like a weight over me, let it spread through me, inky and soft, so I was swamped by it. Not for a reason, not to get something from it, not to go forward from it, just to taste it.

And then I cried. I cried like a storm that had been brewing for a long time. It was like I was the God Almighty rain itself, pouring down from my own inside. Noises came out, sounds I'd never heard come from myself. But I let them come. It was as if I was there and the crying was there and I was holding my own crying in my arms. And the sea was holding me. So I didn't have to stop it. And neither did the sea.

I had no choice but to look up, to become small again, to become big again.

There was the note of a single star: an arrow of longing saying good-bye.

chapter thirty-one

*O*nce I saw a dead dog.

Eddie and I were at Lorne, walking along the wall by the beach early in the morning, playing follow-the-leader. It was my turn to lead. The tide was so high there was no beach in some places, and the waves were crashing up against the old stone wall. I saw it first. A dog's body was being rolled around by the waves and bumped up against the wall. I cried out when I saw it. My hands flew up to cover my eyes. Eddie said, "Oh, Clapot, it's a golden retriever. The poor thing." The way the waves pushed and pulled at it made me feel bad. There was nothing the dog could do, because it was dead. I was mad at the sea and the waves. There's no dignity in being dead.

Eddie stayed with the dead dog, to protect it. I ran all the way back to the campsite to tell Dad. I was feeling important and sad. I saw all the squat wood houses with their beaming windows and bristling lawns and people leaving and arriving with their hunger and appointments tucked and clicking in their minds, and not one of them thinking that there was a golden drowned dog being rolled around by the waves. It should have made a difference. I felt annoyed at them too, even the houses, just for going on, without minding that there was death, for not every now and then moaning or folding in half.

Eddie's dead body was all dressed up in a suit and his hair was greased down. It wasn't even a nice suit. It was a cheap gray suit with a pastel pink tie. No one wears suits like that when they're alive, when they can choose. I'd only seen Eddie in a suit once, for Benjamin's funeral. Before we went to the Castlemaine Funeral Parlor, Mum had chosen some clothes for Eddie to wear, but when we got there his body had already been dressed by the funeral people and we were too embarrassed to ask them to change his clothes. There was lolly-pink shiny material swishing around him. He lay in the pink gummy mouth of a coffin, about to be swallowed up forever, made into air and memory. It looked like a kind of occasion, in that coffin, one that Eddie wouldn't have gone to. Not even I would have.

It was Eddie and it wasn't Eddie. He had gone from himself. There was nothing left except the terrifyingly familiar outline of him. I drove my eyes over his face; I was looking for him, but he wasn't there. I remember there was the sound of sobbing. It was like a song, the weeping, the way one would start and then everyone would join in.

We had to go and see Eddie's dead body, otherwise we wouldn't have believed it. I wouldn't have believed that he was never coming home again. There's two types of believing: one is the believing you do with your mind, the other you do with your heart. I had to let my heart and soul and body know that he was really gone.

Dad and I took Mum to the airport. It wasn't ever said that she was leaving. It was said that she wasn't well and she was going back to be looked after. Perhaps, it was said, she was homesick. Perhaps, it was said, she would get better and return in the summer. But I could tell it was all just being said. You couldn't know anything with her because she wasn't there; she wasn't in the room, she wasn't in the car, she wasn't in her body, not even in her eyes. She stared out of her eyes as if they were a window overlooking another view, a view we couldn't see. She sat in the front seat, looking straight ahead. The radio was on. None of us spoke. Not until we got to those forever-gone doors at customs. Suddenly she became alarmed. She frowned and stiffened. Dad put his arm around her, as if she were a child needing encouragement for a first day at school. But then he drew her to him and held her and I turned away, because it seemed private, a thing between a husband and a wife. And when it came to my turn, I saw that she was really looking at me and she said the strangest thing. She said, "I love Manon." As if she were speaking to someone else. And then my mum just went back to where she came from.

* * * * *

When the morning finally came, I felt as if I was watching something sailing away. Maybe it was just the dark color draining out of the sky. Or it was that thing: the world's unuttered speech, the in-between of night and morning, the place where one thing gives way to another thing and for a moment there is neither. Then the kingdom has no king, and it isn't knowing that counts, it's unknowing. Even as I sat still there on the beach, my heart opened and closed like a fist and blood slid through my body, and I knew I was older in that moment than I was in the one before.

An old black-haired woman wearing a brown trench coat and dirty sneakers came hurrying along the esplanade. She was saying *da da da*, over and over, as if testing the sound of it, but when she saw me she stopped and put her hand over her mouth. She looked at me as if I were a curious object. I was just sitting on the pavement with my feet on the sand. I was a little bit cold from my swim and I had my arms wrapped around me. She said, "Listen, love, you got a ciggie?" I shook my head and said sorry.

"I know you're telling the truth, lass, but you know, you shouldn't wear red around here. Never mind, I can see you're sensitive," she said, and then she hurried on.

Was I telling the truth? Once the truth had seemed like a clear thing, a yes-or-no thing, an easy rule. That was when simple things mattered, like getting a good mark, not annoying your mother, making it onto the A-team, being as good as your brother — but later those things didn't count at all. Later it mattered that you had T-bar sandals, that you didn't limp, that you had a best friend, that you could know something worth knowing, or win the Thin Captain — and then that didn't count anymore either. Then in the end, I thought, it won't matter that I didn't do the things I planned. Maybe nothing ever really matters, you only think it does. And all the notches on the belt that you run around madly gathering — as if the world will count them up and reward you, declare you human after all — they won't count either. All that time you could have been lying there under a tree, under a sky, bewildered only by the beauty above you. And still the world would declare the same thing: You are alive. Yes, you are.

chapter thirty-two

I was suddenly so tired, all I could think about was going to sleep. I didn't want to have too many other thoughts until I was awake enough to think them properly. The problem was that I could tell I was getting truer thoughts by not being able to think them properly. It was as if the ocean was just giving them to me.

I walked my bike up toward the shops. To tell you the truth, I was feeling bad about my dad. I felt bad that I'd run away on him. When I looked back over what had happened, I could see it from another view, now that I was farther away. I saw that we were a sinking ship, Dad and I. We were the only ones left on board and neither of us was being the captain. Ivy was pushed off a while ago, Eddie fell overboard, Mum went in after him, and I sat in the cabin and waited for someone to make it float again. And when no one did, I jumped off too. So I'd left Dad manning the sinking ship on his own. He would never have done that to me. He wouldn't just abandon me, the broken-down bit of family that was left. He didn't say much, my dad, but you could lean on him when you needed to. And Nora, the horse woman, was in love with him. He wouldn't have noticed it himself, because he didn't notice anything much. He was too preoccupied with his animals and too worn out by the love he had for Mum. After Mum left, Nora sometimes brought over a lasagna or some fruitcake or a home brew, which they drank together on the veranda. Now, you wouldn't bother going to all the trouble of making a fruitcake if you didn't fancy someone.

I wheeled my bike to a phone booth and called Dad at work. Veronika, the vet nurse, answered the phone. She said my father would be very relieved to hear from me. He was very worried, she said, and then asked me if I was all right. This is going to sound selfish but I was a little bit happy that Veronika was concerned about me, since Veronika was placid, like a cow, and rarely got in a flap about anything. Did that mean I was worth getting in a flap about? Dad came to the phone. I said I was sorry for causing trouble. He mumbled something in an uncomfortable way, and then he just wanted to know where I was. He said he'd come and get me. I said okay. It just came out. Okay. So it was like that. I hung up and I knew where I was going next. Back on board.

It wasn't as though I was giving in either. I just knew I hadn't quite finished things there. Not yet. I had some vague old notions and they were feeling good inside me. One of them was to get Ivy back on our shipwreck; we needed more crew. She could have the bungalow — Eddie's bungalow. Ivy and I could clean it up, fold up his clothes the way we folded up hers once. We could talk about old times and cry a bit, and then give Eddie's clothes to needy people. We would keep certain things of course, like the record collection. Or maybe we should give that to Harry, so he could have something to remember Eddie by too. There was also the guitar that Mum bought for Eddie as a bribe to make him give up smoking. Eddie's soul once made a visit to me, carrying that guitar. It happened two nights after Eddie died. I was dreaming, but there was such a different feeling to it: a clear, deep, and true feeling, not murky like a dream, not so berserk. It felt as though it was really happening. He was really there: the real Eddie and the real me, saying good-bye.

I was on the oval at school. There was a footy game going on, but I was sitting on the edge, on the concrete step. Eddie came up, he came out of the field, wearing his footy clothes, but he didn't have a football, he had his guitar. I started to cry when I saw him. He sat next to me and I said, "Eddie! You died. Did you know? You died." "Yeah," he said, "I know." I said, "I didn't even get to say good-bye. I didn't get to tell you anything, I didn't get to say what I wanted to say."

What I had wanted to say was how much he meant to me, but we never once in our whole lives talked like that. You just don't go 'round telling your brother those kinds of things; you expect that you don't need to.

Eddie said it was all right, he knew, he knew what I felt, he knew it. I was so relieved that he knew it.

The thing about the guitar was that he had it then in that visit, but he'd never really had it before. He'd never played it, at least no one ever heard him. It just stood in the corner of his room: honey-colored, no scratches, shining silver strings, as if it were part of a dream he couldn't touch. He was scared of that guitar, scared of it showing him he wasn't good at everything. It's terrible to be bad at things, but especially when you're meant to be good at everything. Mum was always saying how Eddie was a natural. But maybe Eddie couldn't live up to the standards he imagined the world had set up for him.

So I figured we should give that guitar to Harry Jacob. We should see it get scratched and bumped and knocked over and lugged through life. Eddie would like to see that happen. Besides, the way it was, golden and unused, that guitar made me feel sad.

Actually, part of my vague old notions extended in the direction of Harry himself, but I wasn't letting myself think too hard about it in case I got worked up, as I'm liable to. So, instead, I rang Ivy and explained why I hadn't come back, and I said that one day soon me and Dad were coming together to visit. I didn't tell her my plan yet. I wanted to clear it with Dad first. Then I went to a café and spent the last of the horse money on some fried eggs.

chapter thirty-three

It was good to see Dad. He put my bike in the back of the car, and he didn't get cross. He didn't even comment on the red dress, though I could tell it made him uneasy to see me wearing it. He said, "Mannie, where did you stay last night?" I said, "Well . . ." and then paused to think about what I should tell him and what I shouldn't. In the end, I told him most of it, except I left out certain details, like my love for the Thin Captain (which I was mighty ashamed of), and I didn't mention the bong and the red wine and the Travis attack. But even me being at Travis's house made my dad feel bad. He didn't say, but he looked so pained that I wished I hadn't told him. I tried to make him feel better by claiming that at least Travis got what he deserved.

"What was that?" said Dad, and I realized that I'd got myself into a spot. I would have to admit what my hand did to Travis's head.

"I hit him." I got around it a bit.

"You hit him?" said Dad.

"Yep."

"Strewth! Why did you do that?"

"Well, 'cause he's a rat."

Dad nodded understandingly, but he didn't look happy about it. I guess you wouldn't want to encourage your daughter to go hitting blokes over the back of their heads with bongs, not that he knew that particular weapon detail. Maybe that was what Eddie planned to do to Travis. Maybe it was what Mum should have done. Maybe it was what Dad wanted to do, but wouldn't ever. Dad wouldn't hurt a single living thing, if he could help it. He wouldn't even kill a spider. I liked that about him. He wasn't such a bad guy.

I changed the subject swiftly.

"Dad, have you ever heard of a D. Wolton?"

He nodded in an absent kind of way.

"I suppose you mean Dr. Wolton? He was your mother's psychiatrist. Why?"

"Eddie had it written down on a bit of paper."

Dad sighed. "Yes," he said, as if it didn't surprise him.

"Why?" I persisted.

There was a big pause from Dad, as if he was considering whether to tell me or not.

"Eddie called Dr. Wolton that night. For sedatives, medication, for your mother."

"So you knew that Eddie was going to her?"

"Only afterward. When Dr. Wolton telephoned me."

"Why didn't you say?"

"Because it didn't matter." He looked at me again, kindly. "It doesn't matter, Mannie. It doesn't change anything."

"No," I said.

He was right in a way. But he was wrong too. It did change something. I'd always thought it was Harry's idea to go to Melbourne, and Harry let me think it. He let everyone think it, just to protect Mum, to stop everyone knowing that she was mad and needed medication, that she was the reason Eddie was driving. Harry had covered up the disgrace, the stuff that Mrs. Mrs. Porrit would have gone to town on, and that was something.

We didn't talk much more on the drive back to Blackjack Road. I stared out the window as we drove up the freeway. I watched the world outside. I saw brand-new suburbs with their grids of brick houses arranged like lines of perfect false teeth in an uncertain smile. I saw them give way to emptied-out blocks where the land got patchy, with a few straggly old gums left in a corner, like the tassels on the edge of a rug. It was as if the land was not sure of what it was, like a person who's neither old enough to know nor young enough to be free of wanting to know, or someone who's awkward and bony and bumped around by growth spurts.

The land slipped, though, without me seeing how, into a sprawling patchwork of scorched yellowed paddocks and lines of cypress and small towns with bakeries and old pubs. And the countryside was there. It was as if the rolling earth and the huge expanse of sky made way for something, as if it beckoned my mind to stroll gently, to gather up and hold the small sheltering of self that the night had tugged and stretched out of shape. The city flared up behind me in defiance, gray and tall, like a hungry lord, aching and bright and waving its flag for more. But I looked up at the sky, spreading out so blue and still, and my mind couldn't help but empty into it. Were all the fragments of knowing that had come to me wrapping 'round me like a warm new jumper? I couldn't say that it was quite comfortable and fitting, but the ill-fit was okay. It left room.

By the time we wound down Blackjack Road and hit the bend where all our houses were nestled, it was dark and the moon was rising. I couldn't help noticing that there wasn't a light on in Harry Jacob's room. Dad saw me looking.

"Harry's gone north. He left today."

"Today," I echoed dumbly. I stared again at the mint-chew colored Jacob house. It looked different. It suddenly looked just like any old house.

"Did you say he went north?" I said to Dad and my voice was not steady.

"That's what Anne Jacob said. He's driven up to Bellingen, to his brother's farm, to help out. His brother's got a broken leg. Then the plan is to travel around."

"Well, for how long?" I frowned.

Dad was wrestling with my bike, heaving it out of the back of the car.

"I don't know, Mannie. He must have got the idea from you, only you went south."

He wheeled the bike to the garage and I was glad to be alone for a minute. I knew Dad wasn't meaning to rub it in. He didn't even know that Harry and I were once, for a moment, in love, but I sure felt rubbed in about it. Were Harry and I in love? I didn't know what we were. All I knew was I didn't like it that he'd gone. I sighed a long sad sigh. I didn't like people leaving on me. I just didn't like it. Why would you bother getting to like someone when you can just about be sure that they'll go?

I couldn't quite believe it was true. How could Harry have left? Harry wasn't meant to leave and I could feel my mind was about to throw a big tantrum about it. Harry Jacob has gone from Blackjack Road, I said to my mind, over and over, as if I was training a dog to sit down. I even pictured Harry driving away. I saw him disappearing into the distance.

It's as though you're a certain shape: You're like a small glass and life keeps pouring its stuff into you, and either you have to grow bigger, or it just splashes over the sides, or even worse, you crack. If I didn't want to crack right then and there, I had to grow bigger. I certainly didn't *feel* any bigger, but I knew that it was right. It all balanced up in a one-minus-one-equals-nothing kind of a way that Harry had disappeared into the north and I would forever and ever be longing for him to return.

I looked at his dark window and steadied myself, somehow. I just looked at it and for once I didn't let my mind get going. I just let myself feel that Harry was gone. My heart was heavy, and I just took it quietly inside with me, as if I were carrying a big suitcase.

I went into my room and sat on the bed. Dad came in and sat with me. I thought for a minute he was going to make a speech because he sat there looking anxious and confused. He rubbed his chin with his finger and sighed.

"Mannie?"

"Yeah."

"I know it's hard for you living here with just me."

"It's okay, Dad. It really is. I wouldn't want to live anywhere else right now."

"No. I guess not," he said, nodding in a sad way.

I felt bad about making him feel as if he wasn't enough. He looked out the window for a while and the quiet between us was large. He took a big breath in and started again.

"Mannie?"

"Yeah?"

"How would you feel about Ivy coming to live with us?"

"Great idea." I beamed. It wasn't the idea that I was beaming at, since I'd already had it myself. It was the fact that Dad had thought it too. It meant he'd been thinking about me and about us, and about Ivy, our lives, the ship. It meant he'd been thinking about something more than his animals. Maybe he wasn't always going to be a passenger. Maybe my short trip south had gone and started something in him, as well.

He was beaming right back at me and it felt that all that beaming back and forth was like a science fiction movie, with rays of white light issuing from our chests, binding us together on the ship, which kept moving through space, toward unknown empires. . . . But then Dad kissed me good night, just like he always did, and I knew I was out of Hollywood and back in my life, in my room, on my bed. At least there were some things you could know for sure, I thought.

I got the book of nocturnes and looked closely at them. I tried to see how the brush did that, did so little but made you feel so lonely. I knew what I was going to do. I was going to copy one, just to see how it was. Maybe I'd paint that view from the tunnel, send it to Harry, and if he liked it he'd come back to Blackjack Road. He'd have to, sooner or later.

In fact, that funny-looking bird that Harry had whittled out of wood was still sitting there on the windowsill, where I'd left it. I picked it up and examined it, as if it knew something, as if it held a clue, as if in holding it I was holding some part of Harry. I hadn't properly appreciated that bird when he gave it to me. I didn't see it; all I saw was a useless thing that Harry had stood still to make. Deep down, I guess I always knew that Harry's way was special and Eddie must have known it too, but that special way annoyed me so much that I couldn't bear it. I couldn't bear to see how Harry was where he was, wings or no wings; he wasn't thinking thoughts about where to go next or how to be better. He was sitting under a tree, carving a bird out of a stump of wood, not for anything, just because the wood was there, lying at his foot, or the bird was there, tucked up in a branch; and together, the wood and the bird gave him the idea. It didn't matter to Harry that he wasn't exactly Michelangelo. The thing was, Harry had nothing to prove. He was at home in himself.

Was I ever like that? Probably before I was born, when I belonged to everything. When I was part of the air: a tree's exhalation. And then I was born. I was there, given a shape, a little squirming body clad in nappies, and howling, simply because I recognized myself within the everything. It's how a piece in a jigsaw must feel once it's cut out and made separate, when it isn't part of the picture anymore; it's just a bit, a howling bit crawling along the old lino, alone, thinking: This is me, the rest is those others. Maybe you never think it, you just know it; and that knowing sends you stumbling into the huge haphazard arms of life, running from your aloneness. You don't stop, no, you keep running and running, until along the way you lose someone and *voilà*, your aloneness finds you.

So, even if you don't know it, maybe you're always trying to get home again. You're hungry for it. You're sent out seeking a way to get there. You sing songs and fall in love; you pierce your nose, sweat, jump up and down, and go pash on an old mattress at the sawmill. You hold close the one you love; you build a house and make a family to go in it. You surround it with a fence and say, this is mine. You make a lot of money and you buy a lot of things; you buy a great pair of shoes, you run. Maybe you paint a picture of the ocean, or maybe you just fall off the boat. Maybe you make a bird.

Home isn't where you live; it's where you aren't hungry anymore.

Right then that little wooden bird was better than any other bird I'd ever seen. I put it on my bedside table, on top of my book of nocturnes, as if they were in the same family. Then I lay on my bed and closed my eyes. Before I knew it I was imagining Harry and me in a big room.

There are long crimson curtains over the windows and they billow out like ball gowns. I am waltzing, with Harry. We're moving like kings. No, we're moving like angels. It's easy. We go 'round and 'round the room. There's no furniture to bump into, no one watching. My feet are in the air. Sky pours in. I'm closing my eyes. I feel his voice touch my neck. Slow, his voice says. Go slow.

I open my eyes and I smile and I dance slower and slower.

unholding yourself

This book was designed by Elizabeth B. Parisi

and Kristina Albertson.

The text was set in Adobe Garamond Pro, a typeface

originally designed by Claude Garamond in the sixteenth

century, and adapted by Adobe Systems Inc.

The display font is Wordy Diva, designed by Chank Diesel.

The book was printed and bound at R. R. Donnelley in

Crawfordsville, Indiana.

Production was supervised by Cheryl Weisman.

Manufacturing was supervised by Jess White.